Cover Copy

He will sacrifice anything to protect her.

Twenty-one-year-old New Zealander Lydia Sands witnessed the hit-and-run of a powerful man's son. Her bodyguard is shot when the killer returns to dispose of her and The Program puts her in hiding. A year later, the case remains unsolved and her handler needs to get her further from the killer's reach. Lydia detests the thought of being close enough to endanger the man who nearly died protecting her, even if it's aboard a super-yacht traveling the South Pacific.

Tyler Whitehall's shooting stole weeks from his memory. Physically recovered, he oversees security for Whitehall Shipping. While on a family holiday, Tyler is suspicious of the woman accompanying them without notice or security clearance, as his nephew's caregiver. Stronger than suspicion is his incomprehensible attraction to her, and his instinct to protect her.

Once sensitive information is leaked, Lydia undergoes re-identification to evade a killer and protect the man who'd die to save her. Her bodyguard has just begun his pursuit, and she may have underestimated his abilities.

Books by Joanne Wadsworth

The Matheson Brothers Series
Highlander's Desire, Book One
Highlander's Passion, Book Two
Highlander's Seduction, Book Three
Highlander's Kiss, Book Four
Highlander's Heart, Book Five
Highlander's Sword, Book Six
Highlander's Bride, Book Seven
Highlander's Caress, Book Eight
Highlander's Touch, Book Nine
Highlander's Shifter, Book Ten
Highlander's Claim, Book Eleven
Highlander's Courage, Book Twelve
Highlander's Mermaid, Book Thirteen

Highlander Heat Series
Highlander's Castle, Book One
Highlander's Magic, Book Two
Highlander's Charm, Book Three
Highlander's Guardian, Book Four
Highlander's Faerie, Book Five
Highlander's Champion, Book Six
Highlander's Captive (Short Story)

Billionaire Bodyguards Series
Billionaire Bodyguard Attraction, Book One
Billionaire Bodyguard Boss, Book Two
Billionaire Bodyguard Fling, Book Three

Books by Joanne Wadsworth

Regency Brides Series
The Duke's Bride, Book One
The Earl's Bride, Book Two
The Wartime Bride, Book Three
The Earl's Secret Bride, Book Four
The Prince's Bride, Book Five
Her Pirate Prince, Book Six

Princesses of Myth Series
Protector, Book One
Warrior, Book Two
Hunter (Short Story - Included in Warrior, Book Two)
Enchanter, Book Three
Healer, Book Four
Chaser, Book Five

BILLIONAIRE BODYGUARD
Attraction

Billionaire Bodyguards, Book One

JOANNE WADSWORTH

Billionaire Bodyguard Attraction
ISBN-13: 978-1-99-003428-2
Copyright © 2013, Joanne Wadsworth
Cover Art by Joanne Wadsworth
First electronic publication: December 2013

Joanne Wadsworth
http://www.joannewadsworth.com

AUTHOR'S NOTE:
This book is a work of fiction. The names, characters, places, and incidents are products of the writer's imagination or have been used fictitiously and are not to be construed as real. Any resemblance to persons, living or dead, actual events, locale or organizations is entirely coincidental. The author does not have any control over and does not assume any responsibility for third-party websites or their content.

Published in the United States of America

First digital publication: December 2013
First print publication: December 2013

Dedication

For my son, Caleb, who thrives on adventure at every turn. You are so precious. Hugs.

Acknowledgements

Huge thanks to my hubby, Jason, and kiddies, Marisa, Caleb, Cruise and Rocco. You allow me so much time to write, and I love you for it. With each book I publish, another dream becomes fulfilled. Your incredible support means the world to me.

To my editor, Penny Barber, you're amazing. The editing cycles are an enriched experience because of you. You rock.

For my readers, I can't thank you enough for joining me, and taking this journey to where imagination and magic soar.

Chapter 1

"That is one massive super-yacht, and one I shouldn't be on." Lydia crossed her arms, eyeing the four levels of darkened glass and sleek white panels as the luxury ship sat proudly in its private berth at Auckland Marina's gated wharf. And was that a— Shoot. Yes, it was. A huge kidney shaped pool glistened from the center of the one-hundred and fifty foot yacht. All the comforts one could desire, except not her. She shouldn't even be here.

"Ben." She swung around, leveling a glare on her bodyguard.

"Don't say it." Ben scanned the marina. "You're getting on that ship and working as a caregiver. No arguments."

"Don't you 'no argument' me. Tyler Whitehall will throw me off his ship, or he would if he remembered me. What happens if he does?"

"He'll have to dive in to rescue you." He smiled then quickly straightened his mouth. "Tyler's one of the best bodyguards in the business, and I still need you somewhere safe, away from home shores. With your case unsolved, Tyler's ship is my choice."

Tyler had been assigned to guard her after she'd witnessed the hit-and-run of a wealthy businessman. Ten days later, he'd taken three bullets in the back to protect her and four-year-old

Jay. She'd never forget his blood on her hands as it had pumped from his body.

"Tyler put his life on the line for me. I won't allow that to happen again."

"Now, he wouldn't have wanted you or the boy to get hurt. That's what we do, guard."

She planted her hands on her hips. "Yes, you guard, but no, you shouldn't get shot. Not for me."

"You're an eyewitness. If we don't have you, we don't have someone to identify Johnny Taita's killer. That's when we find him. Which we will." His look was sharp, determined and inarguable. "You'll have the cover you need once on board with Tyler, as well as a break from the safe-house. Surely you like the idea of a cruise to the Fijian islands?"

She frowned. "That's a trick question. Being in The Program means remaining in seclusion. Not on board a luxury ship. Tyler's wonderful brothers and nephew will be on board. This is their family holiday."

"You'll be in more danger from Nico than he ever will be from you. Four-year-olds, as adorable as they are, are tricky little things. Nico has endless energy."

"Children aren't things."

"Same, same." He shrugged. "All that matters is you're one of the best caregivers I know. I told Nico's father, and he's all for your arrival."

"But he won't know who I am." She wanted to hit him over the head. The man was far too obstinate, and deaf. He didn't listen to a word she said. "Even Tyler won't know."

"That's the whole point of you having name suppression."

"This is impossible."

"I knew you'd come around."

What? She was not coming around, but he nudged her from behind then directed her through the arched gateway and along the slatted wooden walkway. He rolled her suitcase over the boards. Its clatter overpowered the water lapping and sloshing against the pilings.

"What I should have said was you're impossible." And a lunatic.

He chuckled. "We've lived with each other day in and day out for a year. The safe-house will ring with peace while you're gone."

"Peace my ass. I've asked Saria to ride your tail. Damn it, I can't believe I'm doing this." She yanked on his black shirtsleeve. "I mean it. I don't want to do this."

"Hey, you'll be fine. I know you're worried, but you don't need to be, and your sister's in good hands. Stop stressing, and enjoy this break. It's only on offer once."

"Tyler's on board that ship. You know the guilt I feel. I can never forget what happened to him."

"Tyler recalls nothing of his initial Program assignment with you." He pressed a hand to her back and moved her forward. "Simply assume the role of Nico's caregiver and relax. This is your chance for a little time out."

Relax? She rolled her eyes. "I can't believe I have to leave Saria behind. Do you realize twins shouldn't be separated?"

"Brigs is guarding her, and you don't have a choice."

"I could help with her correspondence study. Her nursing finals are so close."

"I'll help her." He increased his pace. "And I think by the age of twenty-one, we can safely separate you two for a month."

"We're not twenty-one, yet." Groaning, she rubbed her palms over her white cotton pants. The ship was so close. Another twenty feet and they'd reach the gangplank, and she was fresh out of arguments.

"This is where I leave." Ben halted and leaned in. "This is your chance to see Tyler as you asked for after the shooting. I know you two were…close. I couldn't grant your request then, but you're not a victim, Lydia, you're a survivor. You must live, even under confinement."

Her heartbeat raced. A year ago, she'd begged Ben to allow her to see Tyler in hospital. She'd needed to see he'd survived.

"Stop thinking and start moving, and don't forget, keep in touch on the sat phone. I expect updates as often as possible." Ben handed over her case and turned her toward the ship. "That's my girl. Now move."

"I am not your girl." Still, she flexed her fingers around the square handle of her suitcase, and taking the deepest breath, walked away from Ben for the first time in a year. She shivered. No, she could do this. A child was on board for her to look after. He was who she had to concentrate on, because her case was stagnant and the inaction wasn't doing her any good. As much as she didn't want to go, she understood Ben's arguments. She needed this break to refocus, and the Fijian Islands, wow, what a dreamy location.

She tugged at the inside of her white blouse collar then lifted her chin and eyed the ship. Up close, the white panels sparkled in the sunlight. Oh no. She slammed to a stop as Tyler stepped out from behind darkened glass sliders on the second floor. He moved across the deck to the stern, and halted ten heart-stopping feet away.

He looked strong and well, his jaw angled as firmly as always. His midnight black hair blew over his ears and brushed his shoulders. The longer length suited him over the buzz-cut he'd had last. So cute.

No. She was here for Nico, not to dance with Tyler again. That's right. Tyler must've moved on. It had been a year. She forced her thoughts under control.

* * * *

Staring out over the harbor, Tyler tucked the tails of his blue button-down shirt into his black pants. The breeze was brisk, the dawn sun warm on his skin. A perfect morning to set sail, on a family holiday he'd longed for. Liam and Nico were on board, and Dylan and Luke wouldn't be far away. These moments with his brothers and nephew mattered as much as his next breath.

Shifting onto his heels, he searched the marina for them, only his gaze landed on a young woman standing stiffly below.

Mmm, chocolate-brown hair, his favorite shade, and so long it touched her tiny waist. And those eyes, the same delicious shade, and now locked on him. Did he know her? She looked familiar, yet not. Leaning against the railing, he called, "Can I help you?"

"Um, yes. I'm after Liam Whitehall."

She was after his brother? "Who are you?"

"My name's—" Rubbing her neck, she glanced over her shoulder then back at him. "Lydia Sands. I'm Nico's new caregiver while you're on holiday. Ben Hammers arranged this job. It was short notice."

She couldn't be Nico's new caregiver. Liam would never employ anyone without running it past him first. Tyler ran all security checks, and had this past year since stepping into the security role for Whitehall Shipping. "I don't believe you."

"You should check with Liam. I promise Ben sent me." Her voice wobbled, a level of distress leaking through. "You do remember Ben, don't you?"

"Ben's impossible to forget. I worked alongside him for seven years."

"He dropped me off." She motioned toward the gated entrance, and sure enough under the intricate scrollwork of the wrought-iron arch, Ben Hammers waited. With a slow movement, Ben saluted him with just two fingers.

That salute was their team's customary silent signal for handover. But handing over whom? This woman? He didn't work for Ben, and hadn't since the shooting. Which didn't matter. The call for aid from one bodyguard to another went unquestioned, and Ben turned to leave, giving Luke a nod as he arrived.

Luke clapped Ben on the shoulder, and then continued toward him in his jeans and t-shirt. Ambling along, his youngest brother adjusted his brown leather duffel over one shoulder, as if he didn't have a care in the world, and at twenty-three, he didn't.

The woman, Lydia. He shouldn't forget her. He gripped the second-floor rail then launched over it and landed on the peer next to her.

She gasped, and her gaze jolted over him. "Tyler, what are you doing? You can't just jump off the side of a ship like that."

"Bro." Luke strode in, one brow cocked. "There's a gangplank. You know, one can walk down."

He slid between his brother and Lydia. "Yeah, I know, but Ben dropped her off. With Ben, one doesn't stroll."

"What's she here for?"

"She says she's Nico's caregiver. Have you heard about this?"

"No." Luke clicked his tongue as if telling him off. "C'mon, Liam wouldn't do that. It's too soon after Gabriella and Mum."

Their mother and Liam's wife, Gabriella, had passed only two years ago. Not one woman had been permitted on board The Idle Dream since then. This was a sacred trip between him and his brothers.

From behind, Lydia gripped his arm and a river of fire raced through his veins. Whoa. He spun and faced her. "What are you doing?" He stared at her hand.

She tucked herself in even closer, and he breathed deep.

"Tyler, I need to get inside."

Her plea spoke to his heart. "How do you know my name? You've said it twice."

A light flickered in the depths of her eyes. "Because we went out. Once."

His heart tripped a beat. Damn, he'd only ever lost a few weeks of his memory, and that was a year ago. He certainly didn't remember her. "Who the hell are you to me?"

"Someone you knew for a short time. We went on a date, and like I said, it was only once. Ben set me up for this job, of which there truly is one."

"Yeah, there wasn't a job going, Lee." He frowned. "Um, sorry, I meant Lydia." Yeah, she'd said her name was Lydia, not Lee. Only why did Lee sound more natural?

"It's okay. I had a child I cared for once who called me Lee." Her lips lifted. "Not that I'm saying you're a child."

"Ah, excuse me." Luke sighed and walked past them to the gangplank. "I feel like I'm interrupting a moment here and, bro, it's almost time for the ship to set sail."

"You're right. Let's go." Tyler held her arm and led her on board as Ben's sleek silver Jaguar revved in the parking lot. "You and Ben? You're what to each other? Are you his client?"

"No. He's a friend and got me this job. I'm not a client at all."

They walked through the opened double glass doors on the second floor and into the living room where two cozy groupings of four white leather couches faced each other. Black and white sea prints his mother had adored graced the walls painted in her favorite shade of ocean-blue.

Lydia's shoes clipped across the polished pine floors as she set her case near the stairwell. She inspected the area. "Do you mind if I ask where Liam is?"

"Below-stairs. Luke will grab him for you."

His brother groaned as he dropped his duffel on the couch. "I will?"

"Yes. Liam's downstairs checking inventory with Malcolm. Tell him we have a guest, one Lydia Sands, and bring Nico." He would see how this mysterious woman responded to his nephew, because if she wasn't a caregiver, he'd soon know.

Luke sent him a good-natured grin as he took off. "I'm onto it, only, bro, you're not to interrogate the girl while I'm gone. I see that look in your eyes."

"Just watch where you're walking." At thirty-two, he'd kept his family and countless others safe, and Ben had dropped her off. Which meant protection was required in some order, whether she was a client or not.

Leaning toward her, he met her gaze head on. "Okay, it's you and me. Now, tell me who you truly are."

* * * *

Lydia needed a sound, realistic plan because Tyler was on form as he'd always been, and she'd clearly stirred some kind of memory. From the first second, she'd sensed it, which was why she'd said they'd gone out.

"We went out for dinner. If you feel you know me, it's from then. Ben told me about your memory loss. We went out around the same time." That should put him off questioning her further.

"Are you saying"—he arched a brow—"we dated?"

"No. It was just one meal. We didn't see each other again."

"How'd we meet?" He crossed his arms.

Okay, maybe he would question her further. "Ben introduced us." And he had, but not the way she'd said. "I can't wait to meet Nico." Where was Luke?

"I'm sure you can't. How'd this dinner I can't remember go?" He came closer and touched a finger to her chin then slowly tracked it along her jaw.

"The food was nice." She swayed and almost brushed noses with him.

"Nice?"

Looking deep into his eyes, she wanted more, just as she had a year ago. "That's about it."

"That's not an answer."

Footsteps pounded up the stairwell, and she stepped back as a man's deep chuckle and a child's delighted squeal traveled to her. Luke raced around the corner carrying a squirming boy over his shoulders. "I told you I'd catch you, Nico. No Whitehall is faster than me."

"Nah-ah, Uncle Tyler's the fastest. He told me he's quicker than Superman."

"I doubt it." Luke winked at Tyler as he lowered Nico to his feet. "Superman can dodge bullets. Your Uncle Tyler hasn't nailed that essential ability yet."

Tyler laughed. "Hey, it was impossible to dodge three at once." He looked at her. "Ignore Luke. I got shot a year ago on duty, and now it makes a good joke."

"Ben told me about the shooting." Unbelievable. "Why do they joke about it?"

"It's the best way to ease the stress. I lost some memory from the time of the assignment, but the outcome was all good. I've been able to reconnect with my brothers and join Liam, Dylan and Luke at Whitehall Shipping. That wouldn't have happened otherwise."

Did he just say the outcome was all good? She tapped her ears. "I'm sorry, your memory loss must be worse than you thought if you consider being shot at as good."

"Yeah, that's not quite what I meant." With a grin, he glanced at his nephew. "Lydia, meet Nico."

She lowered to Nico's level and held out her hand. She was here for him. "Hey, Nico. I love your super-yacht."

The boy with black curls beamed. "Daddy said you were coming."

Tyler cleared his throat. "Nico, after a girl offers you her hand to shake, you never miss the opportunity to get a kiss on the cheek in too."

"Okay." Nico put his tiny hand in hers, and smacked his lips to her cheek.

She laughed. She'd missed being around children. "I'm so glad to be here."

"We're going on holiday, a big holiday." He peered over his shoulder as another man strode around the corner. This had to be Liam, so visually similar to his brothers. He had Tyler's sky-blue eyes, although Liam's dark hair was clipped short, as Tyler's used to be. Dressed in a white business shirt unbuttoned at the neck and navy dress pants, Liam crossed to her.

"Daddy, we're going on a holiday because ships are in my blood. That's what you said, but teeny-tiny ships, 'cause my blood's only little, right?"

Liam squeezed his son's shoulder. "That's kind of what I said, minus the teeny-tiny ships actually being in your blood." With a smile, he extended his hand to her. "Sorry about the late welcome. Luke told me to hurry since Tyler would have begun his interrogation. I hadn't yet had the chance to tell him you'd be traveling with us. Ben only called last night."

"It's nice to meet you, and thanks for agreeing to take me on board." She was here, and now she'd make the most of it. "Whatever you need from me, I'm here to help."

"Great. I appreciate that."

Tyler caught her arm, and drew her back to him. "Nico is almost five and he'll start school after we return. Your professional abilities will only be required until the end of this trip. Nothing beyond. Does that arrangement suit?"

"Of course. That sounds perfect." It would be impossible to have more.

With a hand at the small of her back, Tyler guided her toward the internal stairwell, and collected her bag along the way. They walked downstairs.

"Below deck are the staterooms and staff quarters, and upstairs on the third floor are Liam and Nico's suites."

"Okay." She peeked at him.

"There's a pool and spa on the top floor, and you'll be given a full tour as soon as you're settled." At the bottom of the stairs, Tyler stilled. "This dinner you say we enjoyed. I want you to know, I wish I recalled it."

"I understand about the memory loss." Okay, enough of the

non-dinner. "Oh, nice decor down here."

It truly was. Halogen lights showcased vivid blue underwater ocean scenes adorning the length of the passageway. Caramel-cream walls and plush carpet of the same color became the sandy base for all the blue.

"Thanks." Tyler moved her along. "The crew's cabins are double-bunked, but as you're the only female on board, you'll have one to yourself."

He directed her inside a small, efficient room with two bunks bolted to a blue wall. White furnishings and a built-in set of drawers completed the room.

"This is nice." She grinned, for she would love the area simply because it was all hers and totally Ben-free.

"There's a bathroom, but it connects with the cabin next door. There's a lock on each side, although the other room's empty."

Inside the compact area, she shuffled around the shower cubicle, toilet and tidy vanity, all in basic white. No frills, but she didn't need any. She met his gaze as he leaned against the doorjamb. "It's perfect."

"You seem happy." He frowned. "You appeared apprehensive to start with."

"I was nervous." She squeezed past him and returned to her room. "First day on the job and all."

She twirled in the center of her cabin. Ben was right. She needed this break.

Taken by the round portal window, she skipped toward it and peered outside. Another super-yacht of similar size to The Idle Dream came into berth, the name Star Gazer emblazoned along its side.

"It's one of ours." Tyler edged in behind her, so close.

Unable to stop, she leaned back and came up against him. Oh wow. His solid presence was like a safety blanket of warmth she'd never forget. She wanted to tip her head back, rest it on his shoulder and tell him everything, to extinguish the lie she'd told and lay out their past. Only that would never happen. Knocking that idea out of her head, she straightened. "Does Whitehall Shipping have a big fleet?"

"Twelve ships in total, but The Idle Dream was my mother's baby. It's reserved for family holidays each year. She passed away two years ago, and my father four. I don't usually speak of them, but—" He slid his fingers through her long hair. "Are you sure we didn't have more than a single date? I feel a level of comfort I can't explain."

Her thoughts swirled to the past, to those last moments she'd had with him a year ago. He'd been dressed all in black, shirt and jeans, and her heart had fluttered in her chest. They'd become so close over the ten days they'd been together, but now he was leaving. Tyler had dropped his bag in the trunk of his car and sauntered toward her.

She'd moved in his direction, and Jay had raced past and wrapped his arms around his legs. Tyler had hunkered down and hugged the boy. "I'm sorry buddy, but the rules are the rules. I can only do a ten-day rotation, but Brigs is here to look after you and Lee now."

Jay's jaw had quivered. "Could you push me on the swing one last time?"

"Sure." Tyler was such a sucker for Jay.

"But after Lee does." Jay shot a mischievous look her way.

Yeah, Jay would draw Tyler's departure out, and she understood why. Jeffrey Lawntree, his busy politician father, paid him so little attention. Tyler was a breath of fresh air for Jay, and had never left their side since his arrival. Jay loved that. She did too.

She led Jay to the old oak tree where his grandfather had knotted a tire over a high, sturdy branch.

Jay wriggled into the tire and dangled his legs over the rim, ready to go. He giggled, barely sitting still. "Go, Lee, push." Lee was his nickname for her, one she adored. Even Tyler had adopted it. Only the two of them had ever done that. So special.

Pulling both Jay and the tire, she backed up and let go when she was certain the tire would swing nice and high as Jay liked.

"It's wet, Lee," Jay yelled and laughed as he flew.

She clapped a hand against her mouth as water sloshed inside the rim. Oh no. She'd forgotten to check it first. It had rained the night before and she should have tipped it out.

"There's water in Poppa's tire and my bottom's getting wet." Jay sailed through the air, giggles exploding from him as his red shorts stained darker.

She laughed at his silly grin. "I'm so sorry."

"I can't believe you forgot." Tyler's blue eyes sparkled as he beckoned her to him. "Come and say goodbye to me."

Such husky words she couldn't ignore. "Are you finally off the clock?"

"Yes, but you're still a client."

"And a bodyguard doesn't get physical with his client?"

"It goes against the rules, Lee. It obscures our point of view."

"Rules are meant to be—" At a heavy scraping to her right, she turned. What the…

A man in green and brown camouflage gear and scraggly black hair trailing out from under his black balaclava scaled the high slatted perimeter fence. Beady black eyes sunken within yellow skin, the gaze of Johnny Taita's murderer, drilled into her. The killer from the high profile hit-and-run she'd witnessed was back. Oh hell. No way.

"Lydia." Tyler gripped her arms, dragged her back from her terrifying memories.

"I'm okay."

"Where'd you go?"

She rubbed his warm hands. Tyler was here. He was alive. He had survived.

"What took you away from me?"

"Um, bad memories. It happens sometimes. Don't you ever have those?" How could he not remember the horror of that day? It haunted her and would never leave.

"Life is too short for that sort of thing." He caressed her back. "There's something about you. You said the dinner was nice, but how did our date end?"

"Ah, it ended badly. You never called." She stepped back, only she bumped into the bunks. Then he followed her, and boxed her in. "What are you doing?"

"Go out with me again."

Go out with him for real? Could she do that?

She'd never had the chance back then, and now she was in The Program, one she wasn't leaving anytime soon. But he wasn't her bodyguard anymore. Well, not officially, and not that she would ever tell him.

"Say yes."

She looked into his eyes, and his heat radiated to every inch of her. Oh boy, she was in trouble. "I've moved on. Haven't you?"

Lies though. It was all she could offer him, no matter his answer.

"No. I have a feeling I've been waiting for you."

Her pulse tripped over itself, her heartbeat hammering out of control.

Impossible.

Chapter 2

Striding to his room, Tyler cast off his frustration. No. She'd shaken her head and said no. Now he needed to walk off this aching desire she'd stirred in him. Until the next time. He was not done with her yet.

Pushing open the door of his stateroom, he came face to face with Liam. His brother squeezed his shoulder. "We need to talk."

"Great."

"Uncle Tyler, where's Lydia?" Across the room, Nico bounced on his bed.

"Be careful."

"I'm"—he tumbled over the edge and landed on one foot and one bent knee then picked himself up—"fine."

He ruffled his nephew's soft mop of hair. "She's in the last cabin at the bow. Go, and be nice."

Nico pulled a face and was off, tugging up his blue shorts as he ran.

Which left Liam. His brother sat on the white leather couch at the foot of his bed, and idly crossed his ankles. "Do you want to explain your fascination with my son's new caregiver? It was obvious above deck. I've not seen you even look at a woman this past year."

Joining Liam, he sat and pressed his hands to his thighs.

"She said we went out to dinner, and it would have been right before I was sent to Wellington." His stomach churned. "She's young, Liam. Did I ever mention a woman of around twenty back then? And say yes. I need answers."

"No, and how can Lydia Sands be getting to you like this? One meal? And a year ago? That makes no sense."

"Hell, I don't know. I feel there's more to her than what meets the eye, but I don't know what." He rubbed his jaw, his memory loss never more frustrating than at this moment. "Although I won't stop questioning her until I find out."

Liam let out a low whistle. "Keep in mind Ben sent her to us. And we all know Ben. He never does anything without good reason."

"I can't explain what went through me when I first saw her, but there's a connection, and it's undeniable." No woman had ever gripped him at first sight like she had. This year he'd lived each day with the niggling doubt something more than his memory was missing. Now he'd met Lydia, and that niggle became her.

His brother stared out the long pane of darkened glass, looking lost. It wasn't unusual for Liam to seek his company, for them to chat, and then for him to sit and not utter a word for some time. Gabriella had been his world. It would be her he thought of as they prepared to depart.

Pressing his palms together, he waited.

"It will be good for Nico to have a female's influence during this trip, right?" Liam's words were solemn as he turned back to him.

His mother and Gabriella's car accident was a senseless tragedy, but the pain of all they'd lost, including their father from a heart attack two years before them would always be there. Now though, the ache had eased and the good recollections surfaced and dominated over the bad. "Nico already seeks her out. You made the right choice."

His brothers and Nico were family.

Liam knocked his shoulder against his. "So many memories…"

"Yeah." He rocked forward on the couch. "And we'll make a ton more."

Nico's chatter travelled down the hallway, and they rose to their feet.

"This is Uncle Tyler's room." Nico yanked a wide-eyed Lydia inside.

He smiled. Ah, maybe he had an ally in his nephew.

"Daddy, can I take Lydia to Cam's control room? She needs to see my wheel, the one Grandma made me."

Lydia dipped her head, curiously inspecting his room. He breathed deep. She was stunning, her high cheekbones flushed red, her lips full and a sweet shade of pink. He glanced at his bed, and then her.

"Sure you can, Nico. That's a great idea. Ensure she gets a full tour and after you've visited Cam, come to the deck. That's where I'll be with your uncles," Liam answered him.

Tyler crossed to the one woman snagging his full attention. "Did you have a chance to unpack before Nico arrived?" He kept his voice low, his words only to her.

Inquisitive brown eyes lifted to his. "No. You have a very nice room."

"My mother decorated the entire ship. She had a flair for choosing the right fabrics and colors. Every piece of art on the walls was handpicked by her."

"I've noticed how wonderful they are."

"There's also a montage of yesteryear prints on the upstairs walls of children playing in the surf. They are restored images of my brothers and me from our earliest vacations. Everywhere I look I'm reminded of her."

"You said this ship was her baby. You miss her?" Her gaze was soft, full of compassion.

"Always."

"Yay, Uncle Dylan." Nico raced to the door in an excited blur.

Damn, there were too many people in his room when he wanted only Lydia.

"Hey, there's my sprite." Dylan caught Nico as he bounded into his arms.

At twenty-seven Dylan had risen through the ranks of Whitehall Shipping, earning the position of chief engineer. Tyler's younger brother was dedicated to family and firm.

Dylan swung Nico around his back then set him on his feet. Nico wobbled. "Me dizzy. Do that again, Uncle Dylan."

"Later, sprite." Dylan's gaze landed on Lydia and he let out a low hmm. "Luke said we had a woman on board, but I had to see it to believe it. Welcome."

Tyler stepped in front of her and eyed his brother. "She's here to care for Nico, and Nico alone. Eyes up, in fact, eyes out."

"Bro." He chuckled. "What's with the attitude?"

Lydia slipped her hand around his arm as she nodded at Dylan. No other contact could have calmed him more. Heck. Why did she feel so good at his side?

Dylan's gaze dropped to where she held on, and then rose back to his. "Did I miss something? Are you and her"—he dipped his finger between the two of them—"together?"

"We met a year ago, during the haze." It's what he called it. "And no, we're not." But he'd sure like to change that.

Nico pressed between them, tugged on Lydia's arm and pulled her away. Argh, perhaps his nephew wouldn't be such an ally after all.

"Can we go, Lydia?" Nico bounced about. "I want to show you everything."

Tweaking Nico's chin, she grinned. "And I want to see it all. Lead the way." She looked at Tyler. "Take it easy, okay?" Pulling Nico through, she squeezed past Dylan in the doorway.

Dylan's lips twitched as he poked his head into the hallway and peered after her. "Yeah, I never thought I'd see that."

"See what?" At this precise moment, he hated exactly how observant his brothers could be.

Dylan ducked back in. "You, reacting this way with a girl. Look at that scowl on your face. It doesn't appear I can even look at her. Who is she? And where is my usually calm brother?"

It seemed one lone woman truly could shake a man up. Not good. Or at least not good for him, and that was his predominant thought over the next hour as he fidgeted on one of the outdoor couches on the second floor.

Liam lay on a padded lounger across from him, his shoes kicked off and a can of beer in his hand. Beside Liam, Dylan and Luke relaxed in the same way.

Tyler half-listened to their chatter. What was taking Nico and Lydia so long? Squeezing his beer can and crackling the tin, he let out a deep breath. This was crazy. He should just go get her. He didn't care for her being out of his sight, and he still had a multitude of questions buzzing in his mind.

"Here they are," Nico called as he burst through the doors and jumped between Luke and Dylan. Luke squeezed Nico's cheeks and Dylan lifted Nico's feet, capturing him sideways. They mercilessly tickled him.

Giggling, Nico squealed, the noise flying out over the churning water.

"Hey." Lydia plopped onto the couch beside him. "What a tour. Your ship's huge."

"Did Nico introduce you to everyone? To all the crew?"

"About half of them. You're still here." Sliding closer, she created a level of privacy he more than desired.

"Of course I am. Were you worried I'd jump ship?" He kept his tone low since she had.

"No." She smiled cheekily. "The last thing you'd ever do is that."

"That's right." He rolled his shoulders, relaxing like he should have done hours ago.

"Your nephew is full of energy. You told me he was a year ago, and I believe it's true."

"It's a brave caregiver who'll take him on. He's like a lightning bolt, and tough to keep up with."

"Like you." She grinned.

Flexing his fingers, he resisted their itch to grab her and drag her into his lap. Damn, he had to control these urges.

"Excuse me, sir."

"Henry, I didn't see you."

"It's not often one can sneak up where you're concerned." The older man was one of the full-time wait staff on board. He placed a bucket of ice with fresh cans of beer on the side table. "Would Nico and Miss Lydia care for a drink?"

"They'll have iced lemonade. Ah—" He scratched his head. "Or at least I think they will. Sorry, Lydia, I usually ask. You'd like that wouldn't you?"

"Absolutely." Her cheeks flushed, and she ducked her head.

So intriguing. Now, how had he known she'd like that?

* * * *

Iced lemonade? Lydia recalled those afternoons in Wellington as she and Jay had played outside in the acre-wide sprawling garden. Near the oak tree, a white latticework table and chairs were set, and Tyler would pour their iced lemonade as he watched them. No matter what she did, he was never more than a single step away.

"Do you want some?" she'd asked, although his answer was always the same.

"No, I can't stand how sweet it tastes." He'd glanced at Jay whose feet dangled a foot from the ground where he sat next to her. "But it's perfect for boys. It grows strong muscles."

"It does not." She propped her elbows on the table. "Jay believes everything you say, so take care."

"Well it might, although you'll never get me to drink it, but by all means, keep trying."

With a sigh she eased back and stared down the driveway. Brigs would be here soon for the rotation change, and Tyler would be gone, having done his stint. Ten days, and Tyler had weaved his way into their hearts. "I think we'll miss you."

He cupped her cheek. "Hey, you've met Brigs, and he's used to being around children because of his large Polynesian family. Another five to seven days, and hopefully your requirement for a guard will lift."

"I didn't mean it like that. At least the killer hasn't returned. Jay and I should be safe." She smoothed her hand over his.

"Lydia?"

Tyler clicked his fingers. "Did you hear me? I asked if you'd like me to pour."

She shook her head, clearing it from the past. "Sorry, just daydreaming. Go for it. Are you having some?"

"No. I can't stand how sweet it tastes."

"Ahh, you haven't changed."

"What do you mean by that?" He frowned as he passed her a frosty glass of lemonade, a sprig of mint floating on the top.

She swallowed, and the cool liquid slid down her throat. Delicious. "Just that it's perfect for boys of all ages. I've heard it grows strong muscles."

"Hmm, that sounds like something I would say."

"Really?" She tipped her glass toward him. "Is now the day you'll try?"

He leaned in, his voice husky as he said, "You'll never get me to drink it, but by all means, keep trying."

She licked her lips then took another sip. "You mean like this?"

With a groan, he eased one leg over the other. "Damn, I shouldn't have said that."

Oh yeah, he certainly shouldn't have. She extended her

hand to shake his. "Tyler Whitehall, the name's Lydia Sands. Today you've met your match."

His fingers closed around hers and he swooped in and kissed her cheek. "Trust me, today you've met yours."

Chapter 3

If Lydia didn't allow him into her room this second, Tyler would go insane. He thumped her door again, the wood-framed print on the wall to the left rattling under his demands.

Yes. Her door opened and he was rewarded with her fired gaze and magnificent dark hair tumbling in disarray over her shoulders. Her lustrous locks touched her waist, and he wanted all those silky strands sliding over him.

"What took you so long, Tyler?" Her smile was seductive as she sashayed closer. "I've been waiting a year for you to knock on this door."

He leaned in and touched a finger to her hot little mouth. "My memory lapse has a lot to answer for." He covered her mouth with his, drawing the prized flesh of her lips straight to his. Heat exploded and poured through his veins.

To kiss her…To want her…This should be—

"Sir."

A brisk knock dragged him away from her.

"Sir? Are you there?" Another knock, and this time much louder.

Damn it. Why couldn't he ignore the blasted man at the door?

"It's midday, sir. Your eldest brother sent me to check on you."

Those words wrenched him into the present, and it was not to find Lydia's lips locked on his.

Was he still in bed?

Reaching behind him, he bumped his headboard. Damn, a dream. He snatched his pillow and threw it at the door. It hit with a thump and slithered to the floor.

"Tell Liam I'll be out shortly, and when you do, remind him we're on holiday." Argh, yesterday afternoon Lydia had teased him on the deck with a glass of iced lemonade. And from his dreams, she continued to stir him.

He heaved to his feet and marched to his bathroom then snatched his razor and shaved. Midday, the ship would be halfway to the outer islands of Fiji, the temperature of the topside pool perfect for a swim. Some exercise would be good. He tied his red swim shorts at the waist then dragged on a swim shirt to protect his scarred back from the sun. On his way out, he slung a towel over his shoulder.

As he neared the top deck, Nico's laughter floated to him from the pool. Ahh, hearing his nephew having fun eased the frustration inside him.

Perfect.

No. Not perfect. Blast it.

Facing Nico, her back to him, Lydia wore the skimpiest red and white striped bikini top and peekaboo bottoms.

Whoa. He yanked his tongue back into his mouth. His dream had nothing on this.

* * * *

While keeping an eye on Nico, Lydia bent and gripped the container of plastic floating balls. She tipped them into the pool where he scrambled after them.

It was a glorious day. The sun shone high, the sky a soft blue bearing only a wisp of white cloud on the horizon. The ocean breeze cooled her skin and Nico's laughter soothed her soul. Sublime, until a loud moan made her jump.

Spinning around, she came face to face with Tyler and one eat 'em up stare. He appeared ready to both devour and tell her off. "Ah, hey. What's up?"

"What the hell are you wearing?" Okay, telling off.

"Would you believe, swimwear?"

"I don't call that swimwear. Those scraps of material barely cover you." He crossed his arms with a slap. "I have three brothers and this ship has a full crew of men and your bottom is on gorgeous display."

"I've worn bikinis since I was thirteen."

"They should be outlawed." He caught her chin in his hand. "You're lucky it's only us up top."

"Oh, really?" She cupped one hip. "Why do you call that lucky?"

"Because no one sees you, but me." His gaze shot to Nico, immersed in his play. "You'll need a t-shirt or cover up. Go and get one."

"I don't think so."

"I'll watch him."

"That's my job." She turned side-on, keeping one eye on Nico as he tossed the last ball into the container. "Great stuff. You collected them all."

"Yep." Nico jumped up and down, splashing around. "Can I tip them out again?"

"Go for it."

Tyler gripped her shoulders. "I said I'll watch him."

"Tyler, really. It's just a bikini."

"I don't want my brothers seeing you like this. Luke's got a one-track mind, and Dylan's a close second." He dragged in a deep breath. "Yesterday you left me wanting more. Now it's worse. We need to talk, but not with you wearing that."

He pulled his towel free and wrapped it around her. "Right, that's better."

"Sure it is." Men. Still, she tucked it securely to keep it

from slipping off.

"We'll be on board this ship together for weeks, and I'm not sure I can keep my hands off you. In fact, I'd say that's a given. I want to take this further."

So did she, but she couldn't. Only her mind buzzed with Ben's last words. *You're not a victim. You're a survivor. You must live, even under confinement.* Could she take Ben's advice and live in this moment? Perhaps.

Tyler smoothed a hand over her hip. "Let's talk, in a neutral, private place."

She darted a look at his hand. "Okay, I agree we need to talk. You certainly like to touch, and I certainly like it when you do."

"That's a good start." He leaned in and his warm breath touched her cheek. "Why don't you go and change while I wait for Liam. No doubt he won't be far away." He turned her toward the stairs and gave her a gentle push. "The movie room. Just the two of us."

She walked away without argument, because deep within her, she needed this conversation as much as he did.

In her cabin, she changed into a pair of yellow patterned shorts and a white tank top, left her feet bare and her hair loose. Then she hurried to the movie room, a darkened entertainment area painted midnight blue with a slim-line screen dominating one wall. Tiny star lights recessed into the ceiling set to low, gave it a nighttime feel.

She wrung her hands together. He might be a while. With a sigh, she crossed to the DVD selection housed within a cabinet near the screen.

"You want to watch a movie?"

She spun around. "You're here already? Was Liam okay I left?"

"It wasn't a problem." He closed the door then strode in wearing a black muscle-tee which clung to his wide chest, and tan cargo shorts which looked criminal with how low they sat on his hips. "Find anything appealing?"

"What? Oh no." She cleared her throat. "I mean, unless I count you."

"Now, that's sounds promising." He prowled toward her. "You want to get to our discussion now?"

"If we don't, I might chicken out, and I don't want to."

"Come and sit." He motioned for her to go first.

"Thanks." She settled on the couch of rich blue velvet, plucked the plump pillow at her back and shoved it into her lap. "You start since this was your idea."

He sat and stretched his arm along the backrest and slid his fingers into her hair. "Having you here feels right. Don't be nervous."

"I can't help it. This discussion feels like a long time in coming."

"How's that?" He set his other hand over hers.

Her heart heaved. Okay, she had to be careful. She couldn't say that kind of thing and raise his suspicions. "Sorry, can we slow this down?"

"Sure, if that'll help you relax. Why don't you tell me more about you?"

Well, any talk about her was a touchy subject, although she could speak of her family. She hadn't seen them in ages, but back when she'd been with Tyler, she'd told him of them. "Okay, my parents own a small rural property on the hills outside of Tauranga. My father's in the business of architecture and construction. I have three older brothers, but I haven't seen a lot of them lately. My sister, Saria, lives in Auckland with me."

"Hey, slow down. Where in Auckland do you live? It's a big city."

Couldn't he have asked a vague question? "Um, in the suburbs."

"That's hardly an answer." He squeezed her hands.

"In the southern quarter."

"Well, that narrows it down to a quarter of Auckland's population, what three-hundred thousand?" He frowned. "Why so secretive?"

"Sorry." She'd try harder, and keep to the subjects she could. "Of all my siblings, I'm the youngest, and my birthday's tomorrow. I turn twenty-one." A burn of need raced through her to tell him more, but she shoved it down. "To be honest, I'm not after anything long term."

"What do you want?"

"However long we're on board this ship, but no more."

"You're saying what happens here, stays here?"

"Yep."

"What if I want more?" He leaned in, his gaze dropping to her lips. "That is, after I kiss you."

"Kiss me, and you just agreed to my offer. It'll seal the deal. Otherwise don't."

"And I thought you were nervous." He grinned and kissed her, long and slow, with stealthy precision. Oh, she was in trouble. Then he continued to deal, deepening their kiss and turning the heat in her blood to fire. Every inch of her sizzled, burned, and throbbed to get closer.

She pushed him back and slid over him. "I liked the look of your bed earlier."

"I saw, and I wanted you in it." He tightened his hold on her, and kissed her, until her heartbeat thumped like thunder in her ears.

"I like how you kiss," she whispered against his lips.

"Closer, Lee." He pushed one of his legs between hers, locking their bodies tight. "Ahh, much better. What?" His head jerked up. "No way."

She stiffened. Was that footsteps? "Is someone coming?"

"Yeah, we're about to have company." He fixed her top, which had ridden up with his explorations, then eased out from under her. "Sorry, let me sort this."

He headed for the door as it opened and Liam strolled in. "There you two are. Look, Nico, I found Uncle Tyler and Lydia."

Nico chased through under his father's arm.

"Found, but now you need to get lost. We're busy." Arms crossed, Tyler tapped one foot. "Like very busy."

"This is a public room." Liam glanced at the screen. "Nico's after a movie, and to watch one with Lydia."

"Right now?" Tyler narrowed his gaze. "What don't you understand about busy?"

"Daddy, what about the smurf movie?" Nico already had it off the shelf.

"Check with Lydia if she's seen the smurfs."

Her body hummed with want, but Nico's face glowed with childlike delight, and she couldn't turn him down if he wanted to watch a movie with her. "If it's the latest one, I haven't. Put it on, Nico."

Tyler held up a waylaying hand. "Hey, hey. I'm sure I said we were busy." He frowned at her. "And stop encouraging these two."

Liam slapped his shoulder as he passed him then dropped onto the other couch and kicked up his legs. "No encouragement needed. We'll happily stay."

Oooh, if looks could kill. She was glad she wasn't on the receiving end of Tyler's glare.

"I swear, thirty-two years as your brother has been plenty." Still he helped Nico load the new DVD.

Nico bounced off toward Liam and snuggled up in front of him.

Tyler returned to her and plopped down. "This is ridiculous."

She nestled into his side. "But it's family time. That's more important than anything else in the world. And look, there's

Smurfette. She's cool."

"Cool? How's that?" he grumbled.

"Smurfette has ninety-nine brothers." She chuckled. "That's how it works. All the other smurfs in the village are her brothers. Don't you love that?"

"I have three and that's plenty." Pointedly said. "But I do like the concept of having the only girl in the village all to myself."

She slid her hand over his thigh. "Later. I promise."

Her agreement had him leaning in, his voice a rough whisper in her ear as he said, "No interfering brother of mine will keep me from you, or at least not for long."

She popped a kiss on his cheek. "To being on board."

He shifted restlessly. "And to deals being sealed."

Oh boy, she couldn't wait to live.

Chapter 4

"It's such a warm night." Lydia brushed the sides of her summery yellow dress. Knotted lightly around her neck, cotton ties tickled her back from the breeze coming through the dining room windows behind where she sat.

"We're only a half day out from the islands. Did you enjoy the meal?" Tyler, like his brothers, had dressed formally for dinner in dark pants and a tie. Opposite her at the table, he grinned.

"The fish melted in my mouth, and I'll stake the chef if he doesn't give me the recipe for the white sauce. Not that I can cook, but Saria can." So delicious, and he still had a spoonful of the raspberry and white chocolate cheesecake left on his plate from dessert. "You want to share that?"

"You already had double servings."

"You're keeping count?"

"I keep count of everything."

"I'm full." Nico yawned and slid sideways in his chair.

Tyler caught him and scooped him up. "And you're almost out for the count. Bedtime for you. I've got this, Liam."

"Thanks." Liam kissed Nico's cheek as Tyler tipped him toward him. Nico was one lucky boy with a family who adored him.

Tyler slanted his head toward her as he left the room, his

look one of bedtime promises to come for her too. Oh yeah, she would live, even under confinement. Thank you, Ben.

"Let's play snooker." Luke thumped the tabletop and stood. "Liam, you want a game first?"

"Sure. That's if you want to lose first." The two sauntered away as Dylan came in behind her and pulled out her chair.

"I'll look after you while Tyler's gone. Would you like to take a walk?" He offered her his arm, which she took.

"That'd be great. My stomach thanks you." She patted her full belly.

Outside, the moonlight reflected off the churning waters as they strolled toward the stern. The ship's wake spread out in a white-capped vee, adding to the serenity.

Dylan undid the buttons of his crisp white cuffs and rolled his sleeves to his elbow. "I'm very protective of all my brothers, particularly Tyler."

"You mean since the shooting?" Her heart ached that they'd almost lost him.

"It was a close call. We weren't sure he'd make it."

"I'm sorry." She held her breath, its weight heavy in her lungs. No. Sorry wasn't nearly enough, because if his brothers ever discovered it was her Tyler had protected and taken those shots for, they'd hate her.

Dylan propped a hip against the railing. "Tyler's been more energized since you arrived, like I haven't seen in a long time. He lost a part of himself a year ago, and none of us could quite figure out what it was."

"What do you mean?"

"Between you and me, when he finally awoke after the shooting, he reached for someone. He uttered a name, but I'm not sure what it was, only the pain in his voice was very clear." He stared at her. "Was it you?"

"We only went out once. This thing between us is just a fling." She stepped back and shoved her hands behind her.

Whatever was between Tyler and her would never go beyond this trip. Tyler had agreed to her deal, and for her, Johnny Taita's killer had to be found before she ever truly lived her life. "I need to go."

"Go where?"

"Um, to ring Ben. He asked me to check in with him and I haven't had a chance. There's a sat phone, right? In the control room?"

"I'm sorry. I've made you uncomfortable, and that wasn't my intention." Dylan motioned toward the stairwell. "Ask the captain for the phone. I'll let Tyler know where you've gone."

"Thanks." She scampered off. Boy, she'd have to watch Dylan. He was incredibly perceptive.

After collecting the sat phone, she found a private area in the walkway outside the bridge. She punched in Ben's number.

"Ben Hammers."

"It's me." She sank against the panels at her back.

"I expected a call from you before now."

"You didn't tell me exactly when to call."

"I thought that would have been obvious. I need to hear from you daily." He groaned, rather loudly. "I also need to talk about Saria. Without you, she's on edge. She's even reorganized my closet to keep her hands busy. I can't find my damn black shirts."

"You only wear black shirts."

"Exactly."

She loosened her shoulders with a little roll. "It's not that she's on edge because I'm away. She's experiencing birthday jitters. I should have told you, but she gets them every year. You've got to keep her busy the day before her birthday."

"Birthday jitters? Shoot. Why does she get them?"

Yeah, she'd pinky-fingered with Saria on their seventh birthday to never speak a word of why. "It's a sister-til-death thing. If I tell you what she did which caused the jitters, she'll kill me, and the whole point of our relationship, is for you to protect me against death."

"Right," he huffed. "So I just wait this craziness out, and she'll be all good come her birthday tomorrow."

"Uh-huh, or at least about halfway into the day. By lunch time she'll be like her old self."

"Great." He sounded anything but great. "Tell me how the trip's going?"

She eased further into the darkest area where the walkway light barely reached. "Dylan's very observant, but then so is Tyler."

"Yeah, I forgot to warn you how intuitive they all are, but you'll handle them. Tell me how Tyler's doing?"

"I told Tyler we'd had a meal together, a date before he left for his assignment in Wellington. I had to lie. He sensed some kind of connection between us."

"Elaborate on this connection."

She rolled her eyes. "Do you really want to know?"

He let out a low hmm. "I get it. Tricky stuff."

"Lydia."

She turned as her name echoed up the stairwell. "Oh no. Tyler's here."

He pounded up the stairs and into the moonlight. "Dylan said you wanted to speak to Ben. To *check in* with him. Why the check in if you're not a client?"

"Because…ah."

"Let me speak to Ben." He snatched the sat phone from her. "Ben, you need to be honest with me. If Lydia's a client, I need to know."

Nooo. Why had she told Dylan she had to check in with Ben? Checking in was the wrong phrase. She strained to hear Ben's answer, almost toppling into Tyler.

Would Ben tell him she was a client?

He better not.

She caught Ben's answer. "There's no danger to her in the middle of the Pacific Ocean."

Crap.

Tyler's gaze darkened as he turned it on her. "So, she is a client?"

"I can't lie to you. Yes."

She dropped her head into her palms. Of course Ben couldn't lie to him, and she should never have allowed the two of them to talk.

"I want the full story."

"I can't speak of it, but consider my placement of Lydia into your hands as my favored choice. No one on my staff will care for her the way you can. Take from that what you will."

"Hell." He snagged her wrist. "How bad is it?"

"Her case has top level authorization," Ben stated frankly, dumping her in so deep she'd never talk her way out of it. "Tell her I'm sorry. I simply can't withhold from you. If you wish, give her a kiss from me." Ben hung up without another word. The traitor.

Tyler pocketed the sat phone, his stare drilling her to the spot. "You lied to me. I can't get physical with a client, and with you being here via Ben, it makes you mine by default."

"We've already gotten physical, and I'm not your client." She spun around and left. Humph, stupid bodyguards. She couldn't live with them, and she couldn't live without them.

* * * *

Every fiber of Tyler's being revolted at Lydia leaving, and even though he should let her go, he followed her to their rooms.

She raced, glaring over her shoulder at him. "Ben also said if you wish to give me a kiss, then to do so."

"He didn't mean it that way." He chased her along the lit passageway and heaved her to a stop outside his room. Then he lifted her off her feet and swung her inside. "We both know this can't go any further."

43

She let out a squeak. "What are you doing? You know I lied."

He shut the door behind him. "Take a seat. We need to talk."

"About…" She eyed him.

"Foremost I'd like to think we can be friends." It physically grated on him to say that. "Which means there are issues we need to bring into the light between us. Please, I want you to sit."

She stalked past him and plunked onto the couch. "I'm not sorry I lied, Tyler, just that I got caught. That's still a nice bed, by the way. A shame I won't be using it."

He tapped his legs. "We need to discuss why Ben placed you with me. He may not be willing to give me the details since it's top level, but you can."

"No, I can't. It'll never happen. Nooo."

"Ben's placed you with me, so who am I protecting you from?"

"I don't need any protection on board this ship. Didn't you catch that from what Ben said?" She shoved to her feet, hands on her hips. "You said what happens here, stays here. You're going back on your word. I want you, and you're being an old stick-in-the-mud. So what if I'm Ben's client? I don't need guarding from you, not in the middle of the Pacific Ocean."

"Sit. We're still talking." He had to lay out his position, and she was not getting away from him until he knew it all.

"No."

He snagged her hand and dragged her onto his lap. "Right, take a moment if it's necessary, and when you're ready, start loosening those lips and report to me exactly what I need to hear." He gritted his teeth. "And I'm not an old stick-in-the-mud."

"Trust me. You are a huge Mr. Stick-in-the-mud." She jutted out her chin, which looked far too cute for his liking.

"I want an answer."

"You're never getting one."

"Then you're not leaving." He stood then carried her to his bed and dropped her on it. "I don't care how long this night is, you're going to speak before the end of it."

"I thought the bed was out of bounds. What are you doing?"

He kicked off his shoes. "Getting comfortable."

A mischievous glint lit her eyes and she tipped off her heels and scurried under the covers. "That was a bad move dropping me here after I said how much I wanted in." She pummeled the thick white pillows at the headboard and laid back. "Get undressed if you like."

"Are you trying to turn the tables on me?"

"There's no trying about it."

She wasn't supposed to get in. This was about him taking charge and nothing more. Why hadn't he seen this coming? "You can't sleep in my bed."

"Then let me leave without answering your stupid questions."

"You're not leaving. I have to know what I'm up against." And he could deal with her in his bed for the night, and still get her to talk.

He'd show her.

* * * *

Lydia's chest tightened. Just when she and Tyler were getting somewhere, this had to happen. Still, Tyler looked dangerously gorgeous.

"Mr. Muddie-stickie," she whispered. "You gonna hop into bed? Or should I call you Mr. I-don't-want-to-stick-it." Yeah, that should hit a nerve.

"You'll want to take that back."

Lazing on her side, she played her fingers over the blue spread. Oh yeah, his gaze narrowed and his hands flexed against his thighs. She liked. "Why? Because you're hoping I don't get comfortable and this isn't a long night? Oooh, I'm shaking. You better not sleep naked, because oh boy, that might really scare me into squealing all my secrets."

"That's it." He let out a fierce growl, which sent a shiver of approval through her. "Close your eyes if you're the sensitive sort."

"Not a chance. This is your room after all. Do what you'd like."

He yanked the silver buckle release on his belt then dropped his pants in one swift move. Next, he jerked his shirt over his head, and yee-ha, she was left with the sight of smooth black briefs covering a bulky package she was certain was on the rise.

"Last chance." He slid his fingers under the band of his underwear.

"I'm still good." When he dropped his underwear and kicked them away, her lips went numb and she tried to rub some life into them. Talk about hot, not to mention that rise was now a full salute. Of a very grand fashion.

"So I have to get naked for you to pay attention?" He shoved the covers back then slid in and hooked an arm around her waist. He tumbled her into him. "Now what were you saying about Mr. I-don't-want-to-stick-it?"

Remembering to inhale, she said, "I was wrong. Totally wrong." Because he had one very powerful erection and it lay velvety stiff against her belly. "Quite clearly you want to stick it. Could I ask if that would be in me?"

He stroked a finger down the center of her neck and between the valley of her breasts where her dress dipped. A seriously hungry look came her way. "You're wearing too many clothes."

"I thought we were—"

He kissed her, moving his mouth over hers like a man on a mission. Oh yes. He was larger than life and completely intoxicating. What a temptation. This was exactly what she wanted, had always wanted since the day they'd met.

Holding her close, he broke for air, his breathing fast. "Okay, I can't keep fighting this. If you agree then I agree."

"I do. I'm tired of living the dullest life in the world. I totally agree." She was in. Absolutely. One-hundred percent.

"Ben told me to kiss you. This is his fault I'm taking it literally." Then he laid claim to her lips, sending every one of her last thoughts flying. "I'm going to take your dress off, Lee. Say yes."

She stroked the heavy muscle of his chest, his golden skin holding a smattering of dark hair. "Yes."

He smiled, his gaze heating her body wherever he looked. "I feel like I've wanted you forever. I know that makes no sense, but neither does the fact I'm willing to sleep with a client."

"I'm not your client."

"I'll agree the lines are blurred." He slipped his hands around the hem of her dress and raised it to her waist. "It's been a year for me. Just thought I should warn you." He wriggled the fabric higher, his breath stuttering a little as he drew it over her head and tossed it aside.

"I want this, Tyler. With all my heart, I truly do."

He devoured every inch of her body with his gaze alone. "I have a feeling I'd break all the rules for you. When you're ready to give me the truth, I'll be waiting."

"You won't push?"

"I'd like to, but I doubt this stubborn side of you is going anywhere soon." He spread his hands over her bare skin, skin hot and needy for his touch.

It was a gift he offered, not demanding more from her but acknowledging she had secrets she couldn't share.

"Skin-to-skin. I want to feel all of you." She pushed her fingers deep into his thick hair and drew his luscious mouth back to hers.

* * * *

Tyler was desperate for the same, and if skin-to-skin was

what she wanted then he'd deliver. "Lee." He murmured the name he'd given her as she slid her sensuous body against his.

Hell, she was right there with him, her actions cementing in his mind they would be lovers, for as long as he could hold her in his bed on this ship. And the way she looked at him, with such trust and longing. He swept his hands over her ribcage, his sight fastened on two beautiful lush breasts which were all his. Brushing a finger over one rosy pink nipple, he bent his head and licked. Nice and slow. Real slow. So good. She tasted delicious.

Rising into his touch, she searched for more, pressing her breasts even deeper into his mouth. Ahh, perfect. He wanted more. All of her. He razzed his teeth over the sensitive tip, taking a second before drawing the aureole deep inside his mouth. He sucked. Hard.

His efforts won a soft purr from her, one that tingled his toes and delivered an equal amount of pleasure his way.

"You like that, Lee?" He released her breasts then rose and nuzzled her neck. He drew the soft skin of her flesh into his mouth, creating a nice red mark, to ensure when he looked at her tomorrow, he'd recall exactly what he'd done to her now.

"You're very good at that. The whole kissing thing. Are you giving me a hickey?" Her breath came in short gasps.

"Uh-huh. I don't have a lot of control right now, and you may end up with more than one by the time I'm through." Actually he had next to no control, his cock hammering at him to take her. So, he kept his word, devouring her to his heart's content.

"Tyler." She twisted her head and seized a breath. "I feel like I'm burning up. Is this supposed to happen?"

He pushed the covers off them and nudged his knees between hers. Moonlight through the windows played over her flushed skin. "Yes, but if I'm taking things too fast, tell me to slow down. Although I can't promise I will, only that we'll be doing this far more than once. I'll get it right at some point."

Smoothing a hand over her hip, he caught her white satin panties. He dragged the silky fabric down.

She jackknifed against him. "Oh. It seems I like fast." Her hand came around his wrist, and then slid over the back of his hand, not halting him, but staying with him. "What do I do?"

Her husky words had him reclaiming her lips. "What you do is not hold back. Let me touch you, deep inside where I want to join the two of us together. He moved his hand higher, her hand remaining on his.

Gazing down her body, he spread her folds and licked his lips. Damn, she was perfect, pressing her mound into his palm, her hand threading partially through his fingers. Beautiful.

"Don't stop," she murmured as she arched her back, her breasts bobbing so close to his mouth, he couldn't deny returning to them.

He lavished them with attention, those morsels like sweet nectar he couldn't get enough of. A year was too long.

"Tyler, please, I feel too much." He stroked a finger through her heat and then plunged in deeper to rub a hot spot, which had her gasping, the hand she had joined to his now shaking.

He growled, his balls tightening and his cock twitching at her side.

Hell, she wasn't ready yet, but she was slick and close.

He pushed a second finger in as he ravished her breasts, her soft cries sounding of sheer pleasure.

"Hold on, Lee." He lifted up and seized her mouth as she moaned and thrashed underneath him.

"Hurry," she whispered as she clasped his head and held on.

Gripping her hips, he positioned with care as she dropped her hands to his shoulders, her nails digging in. He stopped. A barrier? Only he couldn't sort his mind to function why. Lee was with him, his mind consumed by her. He pushed through and buried himself deep to the hilt.

Lydia's gasp muffled against his neck as she held on piercingly tight.

"Hell, you were a virgin?" He raised his head. Surely that couldn't be right. She would have said. She should have said.

She loosened her grip and stroked his back. "I'm sorry, but you said what happens here, stays here. I wanted this. I still do."

With one hand on her hip, he eased up slowly, and then stopped. For the life of him, he couldn't fully leave her body. "We'll go slow. Does this feel uncomfortable?" He gently pushed back in, and her lashes fluttered down as she sighed.

"More like…very full." She opened her eyes, a brightness flickering within. "That's good though, right?"

Right now, everything felt good. "You're tight." With care, he moved in and out, stroking into her slow and easy. She mewled in the back of her throat as her pleasure rebuilt. He took in every sound she made. A virgin. He'd never been any woman's first. The fact she trusted him this deeply made his chest tighten painfully.

"Oh, I really like that." She rocked underneath him, moving them as one. "Go faster."

"Are you sure?"

She slapped his butt, grinned and wrapped her legs around him. "Stick it. Now."

He was lost, pounding into her deep and hard, her cries for more sending him over the edge.

"Yes. So good." She screamed his name, her inner muscles tightening to squeeze and lock him firmly in place.

His tenuous hold on his restraint broke, and he drove in, her orgasm taking him too, until he was wrung dry, with no strength remaining.

He collapsed on top of her.

His mind was slush.

Chapter 5

Lydia lay still, not that she could move with Tyler a dead weight on top, but she wasn't complaining. No way. Boy, what that man could do with his hands and mouth was completely insane.

She gripped his shoulders. A light sheen of sweat dampened his hot skin, and she blew gently to wake him.

He stirred. "Am I too heavy?"

"No, you're too sleepy. I want more." She wrapped her legs around him in case he thought to move.

"You were a virgin. You don't withhold that kind of information from the man you're about to make love with. I could've hurt you."

She stretched and smiled, all while clinging. "Ah, but you didn't, and you never would."

"You'll be sore in the morning." He wrapped an arm around her and rolled them until she came up on top. "You've made things more difficult, Lee."

"Because…"

She didn't see how, not when she was so sated and content and…oh yeah, he was still buried deep inside her and coming back to life. And she thought men went soft down there afterwards.

"I can feel you. I like it. A lot." With her elbows on his

chest, she palmed her chin.

"So do I, and too much. How about a shower? That'll help in case you're sore."

"I'm not sore, although I won't object to a shower. You made me all sticky."

He swept her to her feet so fast, her head spun. "Let's go."

They fit snugly inside his shower as he flicked on the water. "I've never done this before. Had a shower with a man."

"Well, you're going to let this man wash you."

"Okay. Sounds like a plan to me. Wash away, and don't miss a spot."

He groaned and lathered up a bar of soap. "Try not to encourage me. Lift your hair." He smoothed the soap down her spine and circled her lower cheeks.

"Can I say thank you, you know, for before?"

"No." He pushed her up against the glass and took her mouth with his, the water's spray catching on his shoulders and jetting over her. He breathed heavily as he pulled away.

"What about, when can we do this again?"

He squeezed out some shampoo and plopped it on her head. "There was blood, so as soon as you're not sore." He massaged it into her scalp. "Tip your head into the water."

She did and he rinsed the bubbles away.

"I'm going to soap your front."

"Well now, make sure you take your time"—she wagged her finger—"because so far, you're going far too fast."

"You're a vixen." His cock brushed her belly, hard and ready for more as he soaped the sensitive skin of her breasts, circling each nipple with infinite care. His gaze and hands made love to her, and he hunkered down, going lower as he ran his hands along the inside of her thighs. She shivered, her eyes sliding shut as his fingers brushed over her dark curls. With a soft kiss against her mound, he let out a groan and rose. "You're clean."

Leaning against the glass, she sighed. "I'm not sure I ever want to take a shower alone again. Are you sure you didn't miss a spot?"

His mouth took hers, and it was more than any kiss that had come before. Her pleasure built from his kiss alone until finally he broke away. "Absolutely." He flicked off the water and opened the door then smothered her in a towel. "Grab one of my t-shirts from the dresser. I'll be there in a few minutes. After I've had a good talking to myself."

"What are you going to say?"

"That you're only twenty."

She sighed and left him. In his dresser, she found a brushed cotton navy t-shirt that was so big it dwarfed her to her knees. It was nice though. It smelled of spicy cologne, just like him. She climbed into bed as the bathroom door opened.

A plume of steam escaped before Tyler closed it then strode toward her, as naked as when she'd left him. The bed dipped as he joined her. "Come here."

She snuggled in under his shoulder. "I hope you didn't berate yourself too badly. I am twenty-one tomorrow."

"I told myself that a hundred times. It should be enough to get me through the night."

She caught his grin, giving him one of her own. "Thank you for tonight. I'll never forget."

"I forgot you once. I'll never do it again." He kissed her, sweeping his tongue along hers with a slow thoroughness that made her wish for tomorrow far sooner than possible.

* * * *

Waking to the gentle movement of the ship was the sweetest, as was the sunshine streaming in through the long pane of glass. It heated her skin and soaked into her. She stretched. "Ouch."

"Are you okay?" Tyler tipped her toward him.

"Yep, I'm great. I always say ouch when I first wake up."

She smiled.

"You are the worst liar. Tell me how you truly feel."

"Like it's my birthday, and I may have worked a few more muscles than normal." She cupped his stubbly jaw and kissed him, one very delicious and satisfying morning kiss.

"Sorry, happy birthday." He raked a hand through his hair. "Now let me take a look. Off with that shirt."

"No." She held the tail ends down as she scrambled from the bed. "There will be no looking. I'll be fine."

"Where are you going?"

"For a run to loosen those muscles." She grabbed her dress and raced for the door.

"Hey." He lifted her, dangling her feet five inches from the floor. "I didn't say you could leave."

"Tyler." She squirmed. "Put me down."

"No. Tell me how sore."

"No more than expected."

"There's a doctor at Resort Island. We'll be there by lunchtime and I can—"

"I don't need a doctor. Now, would you put me down so I can go and dress. I'll see you up top for breakfast. Twenty-one, remember? I can look after myself."

Setting her on her feet, he kept a firm hold around her waist. He didn't appear ready to release her. "You've gotta let me take a peek."

She plucked his fingers away, one-by-one. "Not on your life."

He sighed, raggedly. "If you're not feeling better by tonight, I want to know."

She darted under his arm then out the door, grinning wildly. Oh, she'd be feeling better by tonight all right. She'd make sure of it.

* * * *

At the serving counter, Tyler picked up a plate and loaded it with crispy bacon, hot scrambled eggs and cooked tomato slices from the dishes the chef had laid out. He set his plate on the dining table and glanced at Liam stirring sugar into his steaming coffee. Next to him, Nico playfully dipped his cut toast into his runny egg. Luke chewed, giving him a wave.

"Bro, sit." Dylan pulled out a chair for him. "We need to chat."

"We do? About what?"

Luke leaned back. "Give him a break, Dylan. He hasn't even eaten yet."

"This can't wait." Dylan eyed Tyler. "She had to check in with Ben, and now the young woman in question almost collided with me in the hallway as she dashed past wearing your old shirt, and by the looks, nothing else."

Liam jerked his head toward Nico. "Ah, let's not forget the age of the youngest at this table."

Peering toward the stairwell, Tyler looked for Lydia. "She shouldn't be far away, and if she wears my shirt, that's my business. If she's naked, it's definitely mine. Keep your nose out."

"Boys, you shouldn't talk about me when I'm not in the room." Behind him, the galley door swished on its hinges, the very woman he was after standing at its threshold. She crossed to him, looking incredibly edible in a lacy white-paneled top and cuffed blue denim shorts. After dropping a kiss on his cheek, she smiled at Nico and planted a noisy smacker on him. "Thanks for telling me about the strawberries in the galley. I've got a whole bowlful, and all drizzled with yogurt and honey."

"I love strawberries." Nico giggled, lapping up her attention. "Daddy says we'll be at the island by lunchtime. Can we build sandcastles together on the beach?"

A cute dimple dipped in on each side of her mouth as she nodded. "Absolutely. I don't tell too many people but I'm actually a professional sandcastle builder. I've even got an award to prove it." She held a finger to her lips in a shushing motion, as if it were to be their secret.

"Really?" Nico's eyes went wide in childlike wonder. "Uncle Luke's always fall down, and Uncle Tyler's are too small. I want to build a monster one."

Tyler choked on his eggs. His were not too small. What was his nephew talking about?

"I can't imagine Uncle Tyler's being too small." Lydia shot him a covered look, implying far more with her words. "We'll build them as big as you want, Nico. Don't you worry."

Tyler gulped half his water as Luke chuckled. "Did you breathe in the wrong way there, bro? Apparently *yours* are too small."

"Mine are plenty big enough." He glared at Luke, warning him with one look not to continue with the joke. "Or watch out, *yours* will do more than fall down."

"I believe," Lydia said with a twitch to her lips, "that sandcastle building is a fabulous *sport*, and I can't wait to see what Tyler can build."

Oh, she did not just say sport. "This conversation needs to stop." He shot her a look. "You're encouraging my brothers. They lap this sort of thing up."

She leaned in and her lacy shirt swayed forward, exposing a hint of delicious cleavage to his hungry gaze. "And…"

He groaned and his brothers laughed.

Hell, he was so out of his element with her.

She slid a spoonful of fruit and yogurt into her mouth then licked the tip of the smooth metal as she pulled it out. "I'll give you a break. What else does Resort Island have to offer apart from sandcastle building?"

"An incredible underwater reserve." He bit into his bacon and eggs. "There's a coral reef encircling the island. It's a great place to dive."

"I love diving. I enrolled in a course with Charlie when I

was sixteen."

"Charlie's one of your brothers?"

"Yep. Charlie's the charmer and only three years older than me. Oops." She pressed a hand to her mouth. "Two years, now."

A round of happy birthdays came from everyone at her words, and with a beaming smile, Nico clapped.

Such an innocent at twenty-one. He smiled, thinking of the all the ways he intended to continue divulging her of that innocence. Never had he looked forward to a holiday more than this one.

A buzz of conversation continued around him. Liam promised Nico he'd take him to the beach for the sandcastle building as soon as they berthed. Lydia said she'd get the gear ready, and Dylan and Luke talked about checking out the island's activities.

Never more content than when his family surrounded him, Tyler rolled his shoulders and settled back in his chair.

"That reminds me. I've gotta go call my sister." Lydia scraped her chair back, her abrupt decision to leave dragging him right back out of that comfort. "Saria will expect it."

"Right now?" He nabbed her arm as she passed him. "What's the rush?"

"Ben said she was jittery last night, and I need to make sure she's feeling better today. I won't be long." She cupped his cheek. "Don't go anywhere."

He wouldn't, unless it was to come and get her.

* * * *

Lydia had relied on her twin like her lifeline these past twelve months.

In her entire life, she'd rarely been separated from Saria, and certainly never on their birthday.

After she took the sat phone from the control room, she dialed Ben's number. Where Ben was, Saria would be.

Playing her fingers along the ship's side rail, she waited for him to answer.

"Hammers."

"Ben. It's me." She straightened. "I'm after Saria. How is she today?"

"I've got Mathias watching her. Hold on. Let me find somewhere quiet to talk to you so I can explain. I'm at the courthouse."

"What? Why are you there? Ben?"

"I'm back. I was about to call you." His sharp tone set her nerves on edge. "You wouldn't believe what I've woken to this morning with the headline splashed across the papers for all to see. *Eyewitness in Johnny Taita Murder Investigation Turns Twenty-One, Along with Her Twin*." He let out a gruff growl. "Unbelievable. You have name suppression, but one stupid newspaper reporter just blabbed your age to the entire country. We're only a nation of four million. He just put your head on a platter."

"The media aren't supposed to know the witness' name, that I'm Lydia Sands. That's what name suppression is." Her ears buzzed. Words barely made it past the lump in her throat. "How many do I share my twenty-first birthday with?"

"I did a search through the births database and two-hundred and two people are listed for this day twenty-one years ago. That number reduces to ninety-eight once I eliminate the males from the count, although you and Saria are the only set of twins. It's bad. I found your names within an hour, which gives our killer a pinpointed target. He knows you. He saw you. I even found several old images of you from prior to a year ago on the net. It was so simple and easy. If I can do it, anyone can."

"What are you going to do?"

"First, I've filed a request with the court for the paper to reverse their findings and issue an apology saying they got it wrong. That's only a diversionary tactic. I'll have to look at sending you deeper within The Program to truly ensure your safety. You can't be Lydia Sands anymore. It's too dangerous, and I need to find who leaked your information to the reporter."

In bare seconds, her life had once again spun out of control. "How's Saria?"

"The jitters are gone. Now she's just plain furious. I should have brought her to court with me and let her rip the newspaper reporter's head from his shoulders. She would have liked that."

The noose she'd worn around her neck this past year tightened painfully. So much for being an ocean away from her troubles. They'd just set sail with her.

Ben grunted. "I'm sorry, but I need to speak to Tyler. There's no choice. He'll have to know exactly who you are in order to watch over you until Brigs can get there." Brigs was Ben's right-hand man, and one of her rotating bodyguards. She trusted Brigs as she trusted Ben.

"No." That one word left her mouth with firm determination. "Please, Ben, no. You have to get me out of here without Tyler finding out. I'll stay on board the ship or wear a disguise until Brigs comes. I promise I'll take the utmost care."

"I know this is like a left ball coming at you, but things have moved in a direction I didn't expect. Taita Senior owns a powerful network software company in the capital, and I can't take any more risks with this leak. I don't doubt he'll be all over this. How long until you arrive at Resort Island?"

"We'll be there by lunchtime, and if you're sending Brigs, then Tyler doesn't need to know. I won't back down on that."

"Yes, you will."

No, she couldn't do this again, put Tyler in the firing line, and destroy him and his family because he found out exactly who she was. Argh, why had she even had to witness a murder? Not to mention the son of Taita Senior, the very public head of Taita Software. He was aggressive at keeping Johnny's name in the news. He wanted justice for his son's death, and he was determined to get it.

"Lydia, I'll have Brigs on the next flight to Fiji which lands at four this afternoon. He'll chopper out to Resort Island and be there by six. I need you incognito. You see no one, and no one sees you. Now, give Tyler the phone." His instruction was precise, but not one she would ever follow through on.

She had to breathe. And she had to hang up. With one push of the button, she disconnected the call. She fumbled with the backing and wrenched the battery out.

No battery, no phone. No Ben on her tail.

* * * *

At the dining table, their breakfast dishes cleared away, Liam chattered while Tyler finished his coffee and waited for Lydia. Then she appeared at the end of the stairwell before disappearing below.

Setting his cup down, he rose, certain a soft sob had escaped her.

He hurried to her cabin and rapped on the door. "Lydia." He turned the knob, but got no further. "The door's locked. I know you're in there. Is your sister okay?"

"I don't know. I didn't get to speak to her. Just Ben." Her strained tone caused his muscles to tense. He banged on the door.

If she'd spoken to Ben then he had to see her. Now.

"Open this door." He snatched the master key from his pocket and slotted it into the lock. With a twist, the latch clicked and released.

He was in, only no sign of her.

Connecting bathroom.

He dealt with the next lock in the same manner then swung the door wide, just as she fled into the adjoining cabin.

"Don't ever run from me." He made chase, and twirled her around as he caught her.

Her chest heaved. "Who said you could unlock my room?"

"It's my ship. I'll unlock any room I want."

Her gaze was cold as she raised her chin. "I just spoke to Ben. He said my holiday was over. Brigs is on his way."

Alarm bells sounded loud and clear in his head. "Ben wouldn't do that, not unless—" He stopped and dragged in a deep breath, his air having disappeared fast. "What's happened?"

"I can't tell you. Top level authorization and all." She ducked under his arm and headed back to her room. "Obviously I wish I could have stayed longer."

"I'm not losing you again, Lee." There wasn't a chance he'd let her go. He strode after her.

"You're not losing me. You never had me."

"You're staying, and I'll argue until I'm black and blue that I do."

"No." She shook her head. "What happens here stays here, and I'm not staying."

He crossed his arms. She wouldn't pull that one. He wouldn't allow her to walk away from him again. "I know Ben and he wouldn't send Brigs all the way out here unless things were bad. You can't think I'd let you leave my sight if that were the case. If you need a bodyguard, then it'll be me."

"My bodyguard will be Brigs. You broke the rules with me, and your point of view is obscured." She moved to the bottom bunk, lowered to her knees then slid her suitcase out from underneath it. After running the zipper around, she flipped the lid and stood. She brushed her sides then dumped clothing from her drawers into the bag.

"You're not leaving me, and I'll break the rules again if I need to."

"I am leaving. Brigs is choppering in to Resort Island at six. I'll be gone a minute after that."

"I took your virginity." He had to make her see sense.

She stared at him then her gaze slowly softened. "I know, and you're the only one I ever would have wanted to give it to, only that doesn't give you the right to take over my life. I'm going."

"I'll speak to Ben. Brigs can come, but you're not going. I'll take you somewhere safe if I need to." He made for the door.

"Tyler, you're not listening to me." She raced after him. "I won't place your family's safety in jeopardy, and keeping me here will do that. With my case, there's a murderer on the loose."

"I guessed that. Nothing else would make a case top level."

"Let me go, Tyler. Think of your family's safety."

His heart constricted so tightly within his chest, he was sure it would cave in on itself. "Nothing you say will change my mind. My brothers can protect themselves. You can't."

Her eyebrows jolted up. "Does Nico know how to protect himself? No. My decision is final."

"Who the hell is after you? You can't give me bits and pieces if I'm to protect you."

"You're not protecting me, you stubborn mule." She swung around and finished packing her bag.

He would protect her. No one else but him would. He left, heading directly for the control room. Ben would give him the answers he sought. He'd hammer it out of him if he didn't.

Chapter 6

Lydia had five minutes max before Tyler realized she had the battery. Once he'd disappeared down the corridor, she snuck out her door then raced to his room. She slid the battery underneath his pillow where he'd find it after he bunked down that night and not a minute sooner. Yeah, that would make it too late for him to find out the information he wanted. She'd be gone before he did.

Only what to do about their imminent arrival at Resort Island? She'd have to stay on the ship after it berthed. That was a given.

She sighed.

Why couldn't her life be easier? Why couldn't the Force's detectives have hunted down the man who'd killed Johnny Taita by now? They'd had a year and her testimony, but still no workable leads. Hers was the most stagnant case ever.

Bile rose in her throat as she made her room, an ill feeling that doubled after Tyler stormed in.

"Lydia Sands. Battery now."

She backed away until she knocked into the wall.

"I know what you're trying to do." His breath rushed in and out over tight lips.

"Too bad. You're not getting the battery."

Something beeped from his shirt pocket. He fished out a

small black pager and read the screen. "That was quick. I told the captain to use the ship-to-shore radio to call Ben. It's not private, but that won't stop me from getting the information I need."

"No. No. No."

With a shake of his head, he stalked away. "Yes. Yes. Yes."

Breathless, she rushed after him. "My case is super-sensitive. Ben won't talk about it over a radio." All the way to the control room she pled and when he stopped, she bumped into his back.

Her heartbeat tripped into high gear as the captain held out the RT.

"Ben Hammers is waiting, sir."

Tyler thanked him and grasped it. Pressing the receiver button, he muttered, "It's me. We need to talk."

"We'll talk, but don't be too hard on her. She's scared, that's all." At least Ben ultimately understood her.

"She stays here, and I won't waver on that."

"Nonnegotiable, eh? Okay, expect B. We'll play this hour-by-hour. If things change, she returns."

Hey, hey, that was not the answer she wanted. So much for Ben understanding.

"How bad? I've gotta know."

"A storm brewing. She needs to stay in one...piece."

Tyler tucked her in front of him. His heat flooded her. "Got it. We'll speak later." He whispered in her ear, "Piece is a gun."

"I did say super-sensitive."

"Yes, you did." Turning to the captain, he handed back the receiver. "Thanks, Cam."

He led her to the deck, to a deserted spot under the eaves, and turned her by the shoulders so she faced him. "Are you ready for fight number two? Because I want all the details of your case, and I want them directly from you."

"You are so obstinate." She stroked his jaw, not sure how much longer she could hold out, particularly since Ben had said she'd stay. "I don't want to involve you."

"You don't have a choice. I'm invested because I can't let you go, and this is more than about last night." He captured her hand and drew it tight against his chest. "Something tells me I'm yours. I've felt that way since the beginning. I mean it, Lee. The feeling is imbedded so deep within me, I can't explain it any other way. For my sake and yours, give in."

Her heartbeat plowed to a stop. Obviously contact with Ben would come once they reached land. And well, the truth would surely make Tyler walk away. His safety was all she cared about. Maybe making him hate her was the only way.

"I can't believe I'm going to tell you this, but the sat battery is under your pillow. Ring Ben, and then let me go."

He caught her between him and the wall as she tried to back away. "Now we're getting somewhere, and I'm starting to see how your tricky mind works. Either you just took the first step in trusting me, or you want me to disappear."

"I've always trusted you, since the first time you saved my life. And yes, I want you to disappear. The sooner, the better."

"What do you mean I saved your life?" His gaze narrowed, his hands spread flat on the wall either side of her head.

"A year ago I worked for a politician by the name of Jeffrey Lawntree." He had to release her. It was the only way.

He didn't move, barely even breathed. "I see. Keep going."

"You know the name?"

"Yes, from Ben's interview with me following my shooting. It was the last case I worked on, not that I recall it."

"I've lied to you. We never went out on a date. I witnessed Johnny Taita's murder." Her words tumbled out in a torrent. "The young boy I cared for, his name was Jay." Now he'd surely step back and leave.

"Keep going."

She frowned. Okay, she'd try harder. "I'd just taken Jay to the corner playground. He ran ahead of me on the way home, and was inside when the car came."

"What car?"

"The one that killed Johnny."

"And…"

Her memory from that day returned with full force. "Johnny was leaving after a meeting with Jeffrey Lawntree. His car was parked beside the sidewalk, but Johnny got no further than the door of his—" She shook her head.

"Keep going."

"Johnny was the son of John Taita Senior. Jeffrey had called their firm regarding a software line they sell. He wanted it installed on his home network. I'd never seen Johnny before that day." Ice trickled through her veins, chilling her from the inside out.

"Look at me." He ran his finger under her chin, aligning their gazes. "Tell me exactly what happened next. I'm right here."

She gripped his shirtfront, holding on tight. "A silver sedan came screaming around the corner and hit Johnny head on. He flew through the air and hit the pavement just a few feet from me. His head was bent at an impossible angle. The car, it reversed—"

The image of the killer driving that car would haunt her forever, just as the horror of that day did.

Tyler's lips parted and she focused on him. "You saw who killed him?"

"Yes, as he saw me."

"Give me a description."

She drew in the longest breath. "He was thin, with scraggly black hair and slanted side burns. They were patchy, but almost down to his chin. His eyes were black and beady, his skin sallow, a sickly yellow color. His gaze speared right through me." She pulled on his shirt, snapping off two buttons, which pinged the railing. Skin. She nuzzled between the folds, drawing in his scent to ground her. "It's the same face of the madman who came back ten days later and shot you."

Her gut tied into a hundred knots as she recalled the day the murderer had returned. Tyler had snatched Jay off his tree swing at the first sound of the man scaling the fence. He'd pinned her and Jay to the oak's wide trunk, but Tyler was too late. The lethal shots had already rung out and hit him while he'd raced them to the tree.

"You're doing fine. Carry on." His gentle voice urged her on. "Don't think of the terror you experienced, only of what I need to hear."

"I can't stand this, but you saved my life and Jay's that day, only from that moment on, I was moved into The Program. I have name suppression. Ben is my guard, and I follow his orders." She kissed his skin, right there where she'd accessed. "You bled, and red ran like a river down your back and sides. I couldn't wash your blood from my hands after the ambulance took you away."

He bent and captured her mouth with his, his kiss tender. "Would you like me to show you how very much I live?"

"You don't hate me for what I've withheld?" She'd been so sure. "You should tell me to go."

"I can't. You weren't the one who held the gun. I'll never hate you." He undid the last of his buttons, pushed his shirt off his shoulders and turned his back to her. "Touch me if you want. They're only scars and they've healed."

No matter that they'd slept together, showered even, she'd not once seen his back.

Carefully she traced the three white lines, one at a time. The first was two inches long and slightly off center of his spine. The second was more jagged and intersected the third, which was to the side and three inches long. She leaned in. She shouldn't do this, but she couldn't help herself. She couldn't walk away if he wouldn't first.

Touching her lips to the first scar, she ran her tongue along the line. Licking, she followed the path to the second and then the third, her hands firm on his hips.

Peace stole through her as she stroked her tongue over his skin.

They were healed and he was strong.

She swayed, light on her feet as his muscles bunched under her hands.

"Lee, you have to stop." He glanced over his shoulder at her.

"But I like it."

He smiled. "So do I, but parts of me are getting very hard at what you're doing, and that can't happen. I have to keep my head in the game." He tugged his shirt back on and caught her hand. "Let's go downstairs."

He led her to a private office on the second floor. Nico had told her no one used this room while they holidayed. He hadn't showed her inside.

"Go in." Tyler swung open the door and nodded her toward the blue and beige pinstriped couch.

Light streamed through cream blinds revealing a gorgeous ocean view.

Lowering one knee to the white shag carpet, Tyler bent before a small safe beside the huge mahogany desk. "Obviously you're not to speak a word of your case with my brothers. The most I'll tell them is Ben's requested I go active and to keep you in my sight, and out of everyone else's." He keyed the unlock sequence and removed a gun. Sweeping his fingers over his weapon, he checked the safety and rose. "You haven't answered me."

"You didn't ask a question." She was used to Ben and Brigs carrying weapons, and Tyler had done the same a year ago. Except that fateful morning, his gun had been stowed in the bag he'd dropped into the trunk of his car.

He tucked his gun into the back rise of his navy cargo shorts then grasped her hands. "You're to stay out of sight."

"Yeah, I have that nailed down to a fine art." She sighed as his shirt flapped free at the front. "Sorry about the two buttons."

"I'll find them and you can sew them back on." He tipped up her chin and kissed her. "In the meantime, come with me." How could he have forgiven her so quickly? She'd been so sure of his anger, his hatred, but those emotions hadn't even appeared, not a smidgeon.

They took the stairs down to his room and Tyler shut them inside. He tossed his shirt on the couch then from his drawers removed another and dragged it over his head. His muscles rippled under the tight black cotton. "Are you okay?"

"I'm surprised."

He guided her to the couch. "Tell me what else happened this morning for things to so radically change. Why is Ben now sending Brigs?"

She pressed her sticky palms together. "There was a leak. I have name suppression, but today's newspaper headline says *Eyewitness in Johnny Taita Murder Investigation Turns Twenty-One, Along with Her Twin*. Ben's furious. He said out of the two-hundred and two people born the same day as me, ninety-eight are female. My sister and I are the only twins."

"Your sister is your twin?" He held up a hand. "Hold on. You never said that, not once."

"I know. I'm very protective of her. She had to join me in The Program. She's my identical twin."

"So Ben cares for you both?"

"Yes, because the killer knew where to find me. He saw me outside Lawntree's property. It was why the police put a guard on me right after Johnny's hit-and-run. They were covering their bases, but then the killer returned and shot you, and The Program took over. Ben continued with my case as my appointed Program guard."

"From now on, you remain glued to my side, and abide by any safety precautions I issue. Too much information has leaked, and if anyone wanted to surf the net, they could get a name, and in today's computer age, an image would soon follow."

"That's what Ben said. I know you think I'm staying, but I won't involve innocent people. You've already taken three bullets for me, and I won't allow that to happen again. I'm just glad you don't hate me. I'd never ask for anything more."

"Hate doesn't even come into the equation, neither does you leaving. You're staying here."

"No, I'm not, and I'll fight you on that." She stood and made for the door. "Until Brigs gets here, I'll do what you say, but only until then."

"We'll see, and where do you think you're going?" He fell into step beside her as she walked down the corridor. At the stairs, he moved ahead.

"To collect some beach gear for Nico."

"You're staying on board." He halted her where the glass doors led to the deck.

"Oh, look." A long wharf jutted out from Resort Island, and at the top end of the walkway, a dark-skinned man with springy black hair waved them in toward a berth.

"Here." Tyler scooped up her hair and rolled it into a bundle before setting a black peaked cap from a side drawer over top. "If you're in anyone's sight, keep your chin down. We're only a couple hundred feet from the beach. You go no further than the deck without me."

The captain reversed into their slot and the islander in his yellow shorts and polo with the resort's logo emblazoned on it, snatched the end of a coiled mooring rope and tossed it to a crewmember at the stern.

Wow. They were here. Such a striking white sand beach, and beyond a mass of palm and coconut trees swayed, giving a glimpse of the resort tucked behind. People lazed on the beach and dozens swam in the surf.

"Hey." Luke came around the corner and tugged on the peak of her cap. "We should celebrate your birthday in style with a huge party on the beach. What do you say?"

Her heart lightened, and then dropped. There would be no party, no matter where or how, and one glance at Tyler's stern look told her she was right. "I can't. I'm sorry."

Tyler drew her back against him. "We'll think of something on board for later tonight."

No way. She had no intention of being here that long. Brigs had to take her away.

Luke pointed at the beach. "Bro, something on board? You can't be so cruel. It's her twenty-first."

"She has to stay out of sight, Luke. All I can say is Ben's sending Brigs and he'll be here early this evening. I'm going back on duty and Lydia's fully in my care."

She tensed at the finality in his words. He'd taken her protection a year ago just as seriously. She truly shouldn't expect anything less now.

Luke's gaze traveled from his brother to her, realization dawning on his face. "Bummer." He pulled his sunglasses from the top of his head and plopped them onto her nose. "Sorry about whatever's happened. Tyler will look after you."

"Go and have fun for me, Luke."

"You got it." He winked and shot off.

She faced Tyler. "I don't know how much time I'll have left with you, but I'm willing to make the most of today while I can."

"We'll have more than today. Come with me." He released her and strode to the wide storage trunk to one side of the deck. After heaving the lid up, he eyed the compartment filled with fishing rods, tackle, surfboards, boogie boards and waterski gear.

"I wish you'd listen to me. I don't want to stay." He had to see it wasn't a good idea.

Instead he leaned into the trunk, his cotton shirt rising in the back and baring the bump of his gun. "Could you grab what I pass you?"

"Sure." She yanked his shirt down then grasped the plastic buckets and spades. "Since I'm confined, I'll go ring my sister. I keep missing her."

"Hold on." He pulled back from the trunk and tossed her the sat phone from his pocket. "Call Saria from my room. I'll pass on your regrets to Liam and Nico. Give me five minutes."

"Thanks, I think." She raced to his room and grabbed the battery. The moment she inserted it, a signal popped up and she punched in Ben's number.

"Hello."

"Saria?" She perked up as her sister answered. "You're who I'm after."

"Lydia. Hey, happy birthday, sis."

She grinned. "Happy birthday to you too."

"Lydia Sands, I swear you should have called me by now." Okay, her sister had gone from pleased to huffy in one second flat. "Ben said he and Tyler spoke, not that I know Tyler, but I love the man simply because he saved your life. Ben said he's taken over looking after you. What's going on?"

"He doesn't remember me, although on some kind of emotional level, he does." Clearing her throat, she glanced about his room. "We slept together. Last night."

"What? I'm sorry, but did I hear you right? You slept with Tyler Whitehall? You're in The Program, and one you can't escape from until a killer's been found. There's no way for you to have any sort of—"

"I know, I know. It was just…sex." She'd barely gotten that last word out.

"Yeah, even I heard that lie. I take offense you'd even attempt that with me."

"How's your studying going?"

"And now you think to change the subject. Hello, you've

known me for twenty-one years. That won't fly either." Saria let out a rush of air. "But I have to say, with Ben's looming and all that's gone on since you left, the study has gone surprisingly well. Did you hear about the midday news?"

"What midday news?" Huh, her sister could change subjects quicker than she could.

"Ben didn't tell you? Hold on, he's right here. Let me ask him." Saria coughed. "Ben, I'm talking to Lydia and she hasn't heard about Taita Senior being all over the news. Why'd you not tell her?"

"Because you answered my phone, Saria."

"You left your cell phone on the kitchen counter," her sister replied. "I answered it, because I'm helpful."

"Hand it over if you two have finished catching up and I'll tell her."

"Nah, I can tell her. The bad news will be better coming from me. You have no diplomacy. Sooo, sis," Saria said, "John Taita Senior is demanding justice and that a year on, additional resources be assigned to moving his son's case forward. Ben's on his laptop copying the broadcast to a file. He's going to email it to Brigs in case he has trouble picking it up there."

"A broadcast?" She shouldn't be surprised that had happened since the newspaper's morning headline. Taita Senior was aggressive in keeping his son's name in the news. He wanted justice, and he wanted it now.

The bedroom door swung open, and Tyler marched in. "Is that Saria?"

"Yes."

He held out his hand. "I need to speak to Ben. Can she get him? It's important."

"I heard," Saria said in her ear. "Here's Ben. Be good, sis. Talk to you soon."

With a sigh, she handed the sat phone to Tyler as her sister did the same for Ben. So much for catching up with her sister.

"After Brigs arrives tonight, we'll sail the ship to the secluded cove on the other side of the island." Tyler's words were loud and clear as he issued them to Ben.

What? She couldn't do that. She had to get out of here.

Tyler watched her intently. "Ben, there's no other location that's safer than the one I can and will provide for her. You know it, and I know it."

She didn't catch Ben's answer, and then Tyler coded his response. She sat, wringing her hands together as she tried to make it all out.

Tyler hung up. "It's sorted."

"Did Ben agree with you?" He better not have. Ben knew her position on not involving Tyler.

"Yes." His gaze sparked as he tossed the phone on the bed and leaned over her. "He also said, you're all mine to care for. Brigs holds the secondary position, but will stay."

She stamped her foot. Damn.

Why did no one listen to her?

Chapter 7

Close to dusk, Tyler stood beside the helipad at the edge of the resort tennis courts. Tucked behind him against the equipment shed, Lydia wore her gloriously long hair hidden beneath a cap.

Brigs had called from the main island's airport. It was a forty-five minute chopper flight, and he'd confirmed he'd downloaded Ben's midday news release and that they'd look at it after he landed.

Lydia shivered against his back, her hands bunched in his t-shirt.

"Are you cold?" He surveyed the area.

"Not in this tropical heat. I'm anxious, that's all."

"Don't be."

She drew in a deep breath. "I feel so exposed. There're a dozen people here playing tennis and we're standing about doing nothing. They'll get suspicious."

"You're right." He twirled around, drinking in the sight of her bundled so close. Bending his head, he seized her mouth with his. Uh-huh, nothing remotely suspicious about two people necking on an island full of singles. People hooked up all over the place.

He sank against her, likely squishing her into the storage shed at her back. She was like an elixir he needed more of, and he'd hated their constant standoff today.

Cupping her face in his hands, he traced his tongue around the inside of her lips and loved every inch. Delicious.

"I want more, Lee." Crushing her closer, he blocked her from everyone's sight, slid his hands around to her butt, and lifted her higher. He smiled as she pressed her breasts into his chest and kissed him back as if trying to meld them together. Her actions spoke far louder than her fierce words during the day past ever could.

"I hear something. Chopper blades," she mumbled against his lips.

He stroked the sweet curve of her butt, his breathing and hers loud in his ears. Mmm, the taste of her was an addiction.

"Tyler, seriously. Chopper blades."

"If there's a chopper, it'll be Brigs." He ran his thumb around the waistband of her shorts. "I need to get you into my bed. You're feeling better, right?"

"Yes." She nipped at his lips. "But very coerced."

"I've barely begun coercing you, and I want exclusivity."

"I was a virgin until yesterday. You can't get more exclusive than that."

"No more pulling away from me."

She held her cap as it fluttered from the wind coming off the incoming chopper. "Sure, I'll do that if you stop trying to get your way."

"My way is the only way." The blades whirred down, and he turned. Brigs strode across the landing toward them.

She slapped his back. "Your way is in fact trouble." She eased past him, ran to Brigs and gave him a huge hug. "How was your flight?"

Brigs speared her a look. "Very short notice, and why did I see you cavorting with your bodyguard from up in the air? It goes against the rules."

"You're my bodyguard, not Tyler. He's a pest."

Brigs gripped her shoulder. "Lydia, Tyler doesn't recall you addling his brains a year ago, but I do. I was there that final day for rotation change and saw what you meant to him."

"Tyler has no brains left to addle, but you're welcome to try to knock some sense into him. He won't listen to me."

Tyler eyed Brigs. He was a big man with bronze skin from his mother's Samoan side, his black curly hair cropped close to his head. In his early twenties, Brigs had trained with Ben in the army before Ben had left to build his own specialist firm. He, Brigs and Ben were a team, no matter he'd left a year ago.

"I'll do my best." Brigs lightly tapped her nose. "I'm sorry about the recent developments."

"Yeah, I bet Ben wishes he never dropped me off on Tyler's ship now."

"Something like that." He flicked a glance Tyler's way. "I could take this one away with me now if you wish. There's enough daylight for a return chopper flight. You don't have to be involved."

His gut fisted in on itself. He understood why Brigs had made the offer, but he'd never accept it. Not a chance. "I can't let her go."

"Right, I get it. I take it the sweet ride off the deep end of the wharf is all yours?"

"Yes. The crew restocked supplies this afternoon. We sail on the high tide to the far side of the island. There's so much bush around there, that very few ships drop anchor. We're almost guaranteed privacy."

Brigs adjusted his army duffel over his shoulder and caught Lydia's elbow. "Let's move out then."

Tyler stayed on Lydia's other side, keeping her snugly between them.

Lydia cast a glance his way as they passed couples strolling along the beach hand-in-hand. The surf rolled in, foamy waves rising to beat against thick round pillar posts as they made their way along the wharf to their berth. Brigs strode ahead up the gangplank and Tyler set his hand to the small of her back.

From inside, Nico called out it was dinner.

Lydia slowed at the glass doors and plucked off her cap. She spread her fingers under her hair and swished it. Silky dark chocolate tresses tumbled to her waist. Damn, he loved her hair.

He caught a lock and ran his fingers down the smooth shaft. "What are you doing?"

"You understand why you're not going?" Twining the length around his finger, he tugged her closer.

She poked his chest. "Yeah, because you're a dummy."

He grinned. "But a dummy who likes your smart mouth."

She reached up and kissed him. "I need to eat. It takes boundless energy to keep up with you, and right now I'm low on fuel for our next argument."

He let her go, and she grabbed a seat next to Nico. She picked up his nephew's knife and fork. As she cut his meat, he glanced at Brigs. His friend knew his brothers well from the years they'd worked together. Brigs chatted to them, and then sat next to Lydia.

Tyler came around the table and sat opposite the one woman who held all his attention. His brothers eased into their chairs.

With his legs stretched out, he caught one of Lydia's feet between his, needing the contact.

"What are you doing?" She crooked her head to the side.

"Exactly what it looks like, and a bit more." He hooked her foot higher and propped it into his lap.

Luke let out a low whistle from beside him. "Bro, she looks angry."

"She's looked that way all day." Tyler cut into his steak then turned to Nico. "How'd Uncle Luke do on the sandcastle building?"

"Every single one he made fell down. Daddy's was the

best."

Luke chuckled. "In my defense there were a lot of scantily dressed woman on the beach. So many thongs, and it was most distracting."

Tyler grinned. "Well, you'll be able to build better ones tomorrow. The beach we're going to is within a secluded cove." He glanced back at Nico. "I'm told it has dolphins close by."

"Can we swim with them?" Nico's eyes bulged.

"Yes, but you'll need to wear your wetsuit and a life-vest." Nico beamed.

Luke held up his hands, weighing the left down and the right up. "Hmm, thongs and beach babes, over dolphins and sandcastle building. That's a tough call." Everyone laughed.

Returning to Lydia, Tyler ran his hand over her caught foot and massaged the sensitive arch. "You want to join us and swim with the dolphins, Lee?"

"Lee?" Brigs set his cutlery down with a loud clatter. "Tyler, what did you just call Lydia?"

"Lee. Why?"

"I thought you didn't have any memory recall of this one."

"I don't, and what's calling her Lee got to do with my lost memories?"

"A lot." Brigs arched a brow at Lydia. "Has anyone else ever called you Lee? You know, apart from…"

Lydia caught a hand to her mouth. "No. I didn't put the two together like that. Shoot."

Okay, why was she freaking?

Brigs stood and moved behind Lydia's chair then guided her to her feet. "Apologies folks. Little lady here needs to have some confession time." Brigs jerked a look at him. "Alone, and with you. Obviously it's case-sensitive."

Her gaze darted around the table. "I'm sorry for disrupting the meal."

Tyler scraped back his chair. "The office is this way." He

led her into the room and shut the door. "Would you care to explain what Brigs is on about?"

"I'm so sorry. During your time at Jeffrey Lawntree's, you called me Lee. You and Jay were the only ones, but I didn't think much of it beyond that."

He stiffened. "I think this warrants some form of memory recall, which means you have some serious explaining to do."

* * * *

Lydia searched her mind. What else might she have missed? "Tyler, we spent every daylight hour together, you, me and Jay. There were so many subjects we spoke about, your family and mine. From that first day I boarded your ship, you had this way about you, not with displaying any prior knowledge of me, but certainly the emotional connection was there. Definitely the attraction." She sucked in a deep breath. "I mean, you were totally professional back then. You stuck to your guns."

"Did we ever kiss?" He palmed the back of her head. "I can't stand this memory loss."

"Almost. It was close a few times."

"I imagine I struggled with that." He stepped her back until her bottom nudged the top of the desk. "Is there anything else I've said or done that may have given away any memory recall?"

"Um, when you served me lemonade. You always poured Jay and I our drinks while you watched us. It's not much, but—" She sighed. "Why don't you ever get mad at me?"

He lifted her onto the desk before edging between her legs. "Why get mad when I can get even? I certainly don't feel like sticking to my guns right now. Wanna help me out with that?"

She peered over his shoulder at the door. "Only if that's locked."

He was gone one second then back the next. "You are the worst influence on me, Lee." His gaze challenged hers, and he didn't hesitate to take her mouth, tasting and exploring until her ears buzzed.

"Help me celebrate my birthday, so I'll never forget."

"You don't have to ask me twice." Grinning, he ran his hands around the hem of her lacy shirt, and pulled it over her head. He dipped his head, nuzzled down the valley of her breasts and swiped his tongue across each peak. "Uh-uh, I'd say it's more like my birthday."

"You forgive so quickly."

"Life is too short for anything else." He cupped one mound, tweaked her nipple then bent and sucked feverously.

Wanting more, she arched her back. Always more. His touch sent a glorious shiver down her spine. "Tyler." She clasped his face and brought his gaze back to hers. "Don't ever forget me again."

"You can shoot me if I do." He clutched the waistband of her shorts then dragged them down over her hips, taking her sheer red panties with them.

"Well, we don't need to go that far. Dropping your pants will do."

"You got it." He shoved them down to join hers in a puddle at his feet.

"Shirt." She mouthed as she wriggled up against him. "Mmm, you feel good. This is exactly how I like you."

"Whatever you want shall be done." He tossed it away.

"Then I want you, deep inside me, only I'll never be done." She wrapped her arms around his neck as he dragged her bottom across the last inch of desk space separating them. With a gentle nudge, he pushed his cock inside, just an inch, but one superbly erotic inch.

Looking down where they were joined, the full evidence so sweetly right, she wrapped her legs around his hips and took him fully in, feeling the stretch of tender muscles, but loving every second.

With a deep moan, he pressed his mouth to hers. "It's only

your second time, Lee. We should take this slower."

She rocked forward, consumed by the scalding heat. "Whatever you say. How do we do that?"

"I have no idea." He pushed even deeper, going harder and faster with each heavenly thrust.

"You make me feel too much." She dropped her head back and his lips moved over her neck as he sucked along her skin. Restlessly, she shifted, her inner muscles already pulsing, trying to drag him to her core. "Slow next time," she gasped, digging her fingers into his shoulders. She cried out. There was such pleasure. Her channel contracted around him, squeezing and demanding he join her as she flew.

"Lee." He pulled her harder against his cock, holding her in place as he seized her mouth and kissed her beyond her next thought.

Chapter 8

His heart still pumping at warp speed, Tyler slowly lowered them both from the desk to the carpet, crushing their clothing underneath as he held the woman he wanted to take again and again, and never stop.

He nuzzled her neck, and her answering soft purr of pleasure thrummed through him. Now to take it slow, if he could. He stroked her belly then trailed lower to dip his fingers into her curls. He smoothed his thumb gently over sensitive flesh.

Her eyes jolted open and she pressed her hands to his chest. "Too soon."

With a chuckle, he murmured, "Too bad." Nothing would stop him from making every moment count. He rubbed her swollen flesh, circling her precious little nub, his handiwork earning him a very drugged intake of her breath.

"Or maybe not." She stretched out under his touch.

He smiled and pushed her knees apart, opening her further. "I want to get lost inside of you."

"That sounds like a plan. Don't let me stop you."

He pressed his stiff shaft to her wet entrance and slid home. "I have to learn patience with you, but it'll have to be next time."

He exhausted himself as he made love to her. Sure, he may not recall their past, but he'd certainly never forget a single moment of now.

* * * *

"Brigs," Lydia whispered in Tyler's ear as she lay half-sprawled over him. "We're supposed to look at the files he brought. We need to get a move on." But first they needed to right the room. The desk was jammed against the wall and the chair had toppled over, while her clothing and his was scattered, ah, everywhere. "I think we need to straighten the furniture, and how did my panties get over there?" They hung from the top corner of the safe.

Gripping her butt, he gave her a soft pinch. "You tried to put them back on."

"Oh, that's right. I remember now." She tugged her shorts and shirt from underneath his back, and then crawled across to the safe to nab her underwear.

He remained where he was as she dressed, looking so edible sprawled on his back, the white shag carpet a comfortable bed underneath him. As he stretched, his abs rippled and, oh boy, those powerful thigh muscles she was now incredibly intimate with flexed.

"You probably shouldn't look at me and lick your lips like that, not since we need to see what Brigs brought us." He eased onto his side and caught up his pants and t-shirt then flicked the wrinkles out. Once dressed, he ambled to the desk and heaved it into place. He rubbed the spot where he'd laid her out. "I now have a real liking for this piece of furniture since it's just given me a nice new memory. I'll have this moved to my home office. I want this where I live."

"Where's that?" Easing in behind him, she wrapped her arms around his waist, his words touching her. "If you don't mind me asking?"

"On the hills overlooking the marina, about a ten minute drive to the wharf. It's close to work, and on the same street as Liam and Nico." He turned and looped his arms around her.

"Where does Ben keep you? And not just the southern quarter of the suburbs."

"In a safe-house."

His blue eyes twinkled. "Okay, keep your secret. I'll find out, my way." He released her and headed for the door. "I'll go get Brigs."

She straightened the room while he was gone then plopped onto the pinstriped couch. Shoving her hands under her knees, she gripped the cushioning. He was impossible, and insinuating himself into her life with such determination she wasn't sure she could stop him.

What would she do?

Brigs strode into the room, his brows drawn together. "Hey, you look worried. We'll sort this. I have the newscast, so let's get a start on that." He placed a slim digital device on her lap as he sat beside her and set it to play.

Tyler eased in on her other side and tucked her under his shoulder.

The footage rolled, and Johnny's father, John Taita Senior, stood before several journalists with microphones. Taita wore his customary suit and collared white business shirt, his eldest daughter behind him with her head bent. Surrounding them, more family crowded.

Her heart cried out for them, for their loss.

"Are you listening?" Tyler picked up her shaky hands, laid them on his leg, and pressed his hand over top.

Giving a nod, she focused on Taita Senior who said, "I come before you today, more than twelve months after my son's murder, to plead with the people of New Zealand. If any of you bore witness to Johnny's hit-and-run, or have any information which could lead to the arrest of my son's murderer, then come out of hiding and see that justice is done." He paused to stare straight into the camera. "No more shall you flee."

She shuddered, for it was as if he spoke directly to her.

"Does he know I'm the witness?"

Tyler squeezed her hand. "Information regarding eyewitnesses is strict. He can't get it."

"Perhaps you missed what I said about the news headline. A reporter's fairly given my name away. How did the journalist find out who I was? Who leaked the information? Taita must know it's me. That message was personal, although what more he thinks I can do, I have no idea."

Brigs sat forward, balled his hands and thumped his knuckles together. "When people grieve, they don't always think straight, and Taita could know who you are. He visited the location of his son's hit-and-run afterward, along with his daughter and other close family. Lydia didn't enter The Program until ten days following Johnny's death after we knew her life was on the line. Whether intentional or not, Tyler, Taita's words were a direct threat to her. Lydia has name suppression, but that's no longer enough."

Tyler snorted. "Then we run checks on Taita and each of his family members. We'll see if the leak to the reporter came from them. Perhaps they're that angry."

"It's an angle we should look at." Brigs glanced at her. "Ben won't stop until he finds who leaked your information, but those journalists are tight-lipped on their sources. Ben told me he has to look at sending you deeper within The Program. The killer came after you a year ago, uncaring who he took out to get to you. If it was done once, it can be done twice, particularly after what's happened today. If the killer wanted your name, after the newspaper article, it just got a whole lot easier."

"I understand."

Tyler swallowed. "Is Ben talking re-identification?"

"Yes. It's the only way to give Lydia and Saria complete anonymity. To physically change their appearance, and then have them assume the life of another in a safe location. It's the only avenue remaining."

She closed her eyes and dragged in a deep breath. She could do this. After a year, it was time to move on. Being Lydia Sands wasn't an option with a killer on the loose who had direct access to her name.

She eyed Tyler. "I'm so tired of running. This past year, there hasn't been one detective who's discovered any motive for Johnny's murder. My life is stagnant. It goes nowhere. So does Saria's. She'll have a degree soon, and nowhere to go to use it."

His fingers dug into hers. "The option has only just been put before you."

"There are seven billion people on this planet, and I could live just about anywhere on it. I've always held off on the thought of a new name and undergoing full re-identification because I thought Taita's case would be solved." She turned to Brigs. "I'm with Ben on this."

His gaze held deep compassion. "Twins are too noticeable together. You and Saria would be separated."

Her hands shook, and she clasped them together, thinking only of her sister. "But we'd have a life to live as we don't have now. Saria would want that, as I do."

"You can't come into contact with anyone who knew you in your past life. You'd have to be absolutely certain this is the path you want to take."

Tyler caught her shoulders and turned her toward him. "It's too sudden."

"No, whether I've had a year to consider this, or a day, my desire remains the same." She eased up and paced the room. "My sister's life is precious to me. Both of us want to live. I'll speak with her."

Tyler let out a low growl as he joined her and took her elbow. "Excuse us, Brigs. This won't take long."

"You can't change my mind."

He led her from the room, pulled the office door shut and checked both directions of the passageway. "I need more time to see if I can expand on your options."

"I'm out of options."

He stroked her cheek. "I'll come up with something, and in the meantime you'll stay here. I want you to move in with me."

"What? Tyler, you can't ask me that. You have your family to think of. No." She stepped back. "I won't pull you into my problems. We've already discussed this."

He took a jagged breath. "Will you give me some time?"

"Don't ask that of me. I'm going to make that call now, and you can't stop me." She fled. Her decision was made. She'd speak to Saria and Ben, and set into motion what had to be done.

* * * *

Tyler returned to the office, ticking over all possible avenues open to him. "She's very stubborn." He sat with Brigs, and dropped his head into his opened palms. "I have no recollection from the time she and I first met, except emotionally I've retained what was forged between us. I can't let her go."

"You're in deep with her." Brigs squeezed his shoulder. "Mate, I'm sorry."

He raised his head. "Then arm me with as much information as you can. Whatever you haven't told me about her case, I need to know."

"Let's start."

An hour later, his mind reeled with all he'd taken in. Brigs had warned him throughout the telling that so far, no concrete leads had come from any of the information he and Ben had gathered, although with the new information at least he had a wider grasp.

"Why don't we break from this until morning," Brigs offered as he rose to his feet.

"Sure. I'll show you to your cabin." As it was, he needed to see Lydia. She hadn't agreed to move in with him, but she was.

After entering her deserted room, he grabbed her bag, which she'd tossed her clothes into that morning then left Brigs to settle in so she couldn't escape back to it.

Down the hallway, she walked toward him then slowed as her gaze dropped to her case in his hands. "What am I going to do with you?" She shook her head, tut-tutting under her breath.

"You'd already packed." He slid a hand around her waist and led her to his room. "I'm simply moving your belongings from one room to another, and I'll show you exactly what you can do with me." He closed his bedroom door and flicked the lock.

She set her hands on her hips. "Ah, is that to keep me in, or others out?"

"Both." He dumped her bag beside his drawers and unzipped it. "What did Saria say?"

"We had a long talk, and she said yes. She'll let me go through re-identification first, and follow as soon as she sits her finals. They're in just a few weeks." She stepped up to him. "Ben will place my application tomorrow, although he said it might take a few days for all the arrangements to be made. He told me to hold tight and wait."

Gritting his teeth, he opened his bottom drawer and piled her clothing in. "He approved of it all, this fast?" He'd have words with Ben. She should be with him.

"Of course. It was his idea to start with." She gripped his arm. "I never said I'd move in with you, and now you're unpacking for me?"

"Lee." He dragged her into his arms. "I want you here, no matter the length of time." He lifted her and laid her on his bed. Stealthily, he moved in to lie over top.

"I know you do. Oh, do you feel that? The ship's moving." Cranking her head to the side, she peered out the windows where the lights of the resort flickered.

"We're sailing to the far side of the island. There's a quiet cove, and it'll be the safest place for you."

"I hadn't forgotten." She slid her hand down his chest and

played her fingers over the ridges of his abs under his shirt. "As long as we're *all* safe, I can deal with it, for a short while."

He lowered his forehead to hers. "Since you insist on going through re-identification, I need to be able to track you once you go under. I'm giving you fair warning now."

"Ah, excuse me. That sounds highly illegal. The whole point of re-identification is so no one can find me."

"Yes, but I'm not a threat to you, and only you and I will know what I've done."

"And what will that be? Ex-act-ly?"

"By track, I mean I'll place under your skin a very small tagged chip. It's like a GPS system, but it'll have a direct signal to me."

"And…" Her gaze narrowed.

He rubbed his cheek against hers. "I'll be able to check in with you, no matter where you are in the world. We can hardly have an exclusive relationship without there being some form of relationship."

"Sooo, you're asking me to go against the rules of re-identification?" She gave him a look that said she wasn't going to agree.

"You're very stubborn, but I happen to be twice as bad. Whether you agree or not, I'm going ahead with it."

"Hmm, and how do you propose to source this chip and then imbed it?"

"Bodyguards use tag and trackers when necessary, so I'm more than familiar with them. The device I'm speaking of can be ordered and delivered to the resort."

"And the imbedding part?" Her gaze was sharp, incredibly watchful.

"I won't lose you, and I'll be careful. It'll be a small spot near your hip, with one or two butterfly stitches to hold it until it heals." He pushed off the bed and drew her to her feet. "Which means I need to use the sat phone and place an order to the

American firm I've used in the past. We're in the middle of the back-waters of the South Pacific, and I want that package pronto."

"You do realize I'm not going to agree to this, right?"

"I'll bring you around." He kissed her on the lips.

No one would take her from him. Not ever again.

He'd make certain of it.

Chapter 9

Tyler was impatient, pacing the pristine white sand of the curved cove after finally receiving notification his courier package had been delivered to the resort.

He should have had it forty-eight hours ago. Five days they'd been here. It was unacceptable he'd had to wait so long.

For miles either side, the land was all high, jagged cliff faces with only one single track leading inland through the jungle. Near the beginning of the track, Liam had slung a colorful hammock and rested, his straw hat drawn low over his head as he rocked in the gentle breeze.

He raised a hand and saluted to Brigs as he finished his swim. With the package ready to pick up, he had to go.

"What's up?" Lydia glanced sideways at him as she rose from helping Nico collect a bucketful of shells for their latest sandcastle. She walked toward him with her purple string bikini peeking through the white cotton of one of his long, white shirts.

Tapping the sat phone in his hand, he said, "If I leave now, I'll be back within the hour, with the *you know what*." He dragged her against him and her silky hair slipped over his arms.

"You're still serious about this?" She wrapped her arms around his waist.

"More than ever. It'll be painless."

"I doubt that."

"I promise to make it up to you afterward." He nuzzled her neck, aiming to sway with seduction. "So, is that a yes?"

"The only embedding that will occur between us will not be by chip." She arched her neck for more. "You never take no for an answer. I'll have to train that out of you."

"You can't do that if I can't find you." He smiled. "Which sounds like an actual agreement to me. Brigs is almost here. I'll have him watch you." With a quick kiss, he left her before she could object again. After jogging over to one of the two beached inflatables, he removed the stowed basket of food and towels and passed them to Brigs.

"I take it you're off somewhere?" Brigs set the basket on the sand then used one of the towels and dried himself.

"Yeah, to the resort. I'll only be an hour. I need you to watch Lydia for me."

"Of course. You don't even have to ask, except this is not like you. We've been here five days, and you haven't left her once. Why are you heading to the resort?"

Tyler heaved the inflatable further into the water, jumped in and revved the motor. "Shipping business. Nothing to worry about." He cringed at his lie, but he couldn't spill the details to Brigs. What he was about to do was private and between him and Lydia, and there would be no stopping him. He needed his woman tagged. He wouldn't have her undergo re-identification without some way of finding her. It'd never happen.

* * * *

"Thanks for bringing the food basket. Right here is fine, Brigs." Lydia pointed to a nice dry spot near her and Nico's sandcastle. She squeezed Nico's shoulder. "Why don't you go and wake up Daddy. He's had a long enough nap."

With a grin, Nico sprinted to the tree line. Liam had one foot dangling over the side of the hammock, and Nico grabbed his toes. Liam chuckled, snagged Nico up and dragged him in with him. Liam adored his son, and her heart lightened, bubbling with joy at witnessing such devotion. It was another precious moment she couldn't get enough of. Being around Tyler was wonderful, but sharing this time with him and his brothers, even better.

"Do you miss your family?" Brigs sat on the navy and red striped blanket which he'd spread for them. "It has to be hard."

"Yeah, but I've handled it." She sat and twiddled her fingers. "It's better knowing they're alive and safe, than never seeing them again because something bad happened." Like it had with Tyler. She would never place him in the firing line again.

"Ben will never give up trying to find the killer." Brigs rested his elbows on his propped knees.

"I know. Living with Ben for this past year has taught me he never stops until he gets what he wants. Tyler's the same."

"It comes with the business. Bodyguards like to protect what's theirs."

"Do they ever." She smiled and glanced out at sea. Dylan and Luke skimmed around the cove on their Wave Runners. They'd been in and out all morning, exploring along this side of the island.

They came in, beached their machines, and then strode their way.

"Hey guys, where's Tyler?" Dylan fell to the ground beside her. Sand stuck to his black wetsuit, as it did Luke's when he dropped in to take a place on her other side. Tyler's brothers were as protective of her as he was. It was as if they all fed off the same emotions.

"He's gone on a quick trip to the resort." She rubbed her chest, missing him more than she liked. Goodness, he hadn't even been gone ten minutes and she was stressing over it.

Dylan eased his sunglasses up with one finger and eyed her. "It must have been urgent for him to leave."

"No, just shipping business. He'll only be gone an hour." To affect calm, she raised the lid of the basket and pulled out some food. "Help yourselves, guys."

With a grin, Luke snatched the container of chicken legs. "Ahh, with Tyler gone, there'll be all the more for me to eat."

She made a space for Nico as he skipped over, tugging on Liam's hand. Liam halted mid-step as he checked over his shoulder toward the bush. "I think I hear something. A chopper?"

Brigs was on his feet, tilting his head in the same direction. "I hear it too." He scrutinized her. "I'm sorry, Lydia. It's bad timing Tyler had to leave, particularly since I had to keep this piece of information from him, but Ben confirmed with me your extraction team would arrive at 1200 hours."

Liam snarled under his breath. "Why does Lydia need an extraction team? What the hell's going on?"

"I'm sorry, Liam. I hate to let you down, but you know I can't speak of my circumstances. This is just what has to be." She stood as the chopper flew over the bush line. It swept out and circled The Idle Dream anchored in the deep. Chills raced down her spine. No. She could deal with this. She stepped up to Liam and the little boy she completely adored. "I'll miss your birthday, Nico, but I won't forget. You'll always be in my thoughts."

Tears welled in his eyes and he turned his head into Liam's side. "I don't want Lydia to go, Daddy. She has to stay. Tell her to stay."

His sobs squeezed her heart. "You mean the world to me, Nico." He threw himself into her arms. She held him tight, their tears mingling. "I want you to look after Uncle Tyler for me. That's really important."

With a sob, he clutched her closer, and her chest near caved in on itself. Like Tyler, Nico had weaved his way into her heart.

"Time to go." Brigs rubbed her arm.

She handed Nico over and backed away from them all. The chopper hovered in, cleared the water line, and landed. Two men dressed in black on black jumped from the cab and motioned her and Brigs over.

One had a buzz-cut, his inky-black hair like stubble on the top of his head. He extended his hand, his gaze a vivid green. "The name's Gene Gilchrist. My pilot and partner is Haden Gunnar. You can call him Gunnar."

Her hand shook as she took his. "I'd like to say it's nice to meet you both." Even though this was what she wanted, it completely tore her world apart. Her life from this moment would never be the same.

Gunnar dipped his navy cap low on his head, a few locks of blond peeking from underneath. "Re-identification is never an easy alternative." He motioned toward the chopper. "In the back seat is a sealed bag containing your prerequisite clothing. You'll need to remove every item you're wearing and store it in the bag after changing. Take as long as you need."

This was real. This was happening now.

She teetered forward, pushing her legs toward the chopper. Gunnar opened the cab's back door and helped her in. "The glass is darkened. We'll wait outside."

"Okay." The clear sealed bag seemed to pulse with a life of its own. With numb fingers, she withdrew a black t-shirt, black drawstring pants, underwear and a black cap. All were cotton, all nondescript.

She changed and folded up her bikini then placed it in the bag. Bringing Tyler's white shirt to her nose, she drew in a deep breath, wishing she could keep at least this one thing of his. Goodness, he never let her wear a swimsuit without one of his shirts as a cover-up.

Her tears dripped onto the fabric. She was strong. She could do this. She shoved it into the bag.

Once out of the chopper, she handed the bag to Gilchrist who did a quick check and passed it to Brigs. "Dispose of these and the rest of her possessions in a timely manner. We'll provide all she needs, and once we're airborne, I'll send a message to Hammers informing him the handover is done."

Her chest pounded. She wouldn't get another chance to speak to Saria and her family, even Ben. Certainly not Tyler. This was it.

Brigs engulfed her in his arms. "I'll let them know you wished for more. All of them."

"Tell Saria I love her. Tell my family too. Tell—"

The pain of losing Tyler ripped her heart in two. She wiped at the tears streaming down her cheeks.

"Tell Tyler I want him to be happy, and no matter where I am in the world, I'll always have him close."

She backed up then clambered into the rear as Gunnar took the front seat and negotiated the controls. He pointed to a set of headgear on the hook in front of her. She grasped the earmuffs and stuffed them on.

Out the window, Brigs jogged back to the others. Luke raised a hand to her, and Dylan kicked at the sand underfoot. Nico was in Liam's arms, his head burrowed into his father's shoulder, his back bumping up and down. Liam scowled.

As the chopper lifted higher, she craned her head back until they became specks in the distance.

"Did you catch that?"

"What?" She jumped as Gilchrist spoke through the headset.

"I'll begin again. I understand this is difficult." He nodded. "We have a private jet waiting to dispatch at Nadi airport. In the black pouch at the base of your seat is your new birth certificate, passport, driver's license, credit card and bank account details. There's a folder with other relevant information. Take this flight time to become familiar with your new identity, and your history. Any questions so far?"

"No." Wringing her hands together, she tried to restore some feeling to her fingers. Too cold.

Gilchrist reached across and squeezed her hands. "It's all right. It's quite normal to go into shock. The black pouch is at the base of your seat. When you're ready, take a look through it. You'll see I'm your primary handler, and my details are in your pack. To begin with, employment and a new family member are provided within the environment Gunnar and I'll take you to. That family member will be Mr. Ronson Brown, retired ex-Force. You are now his niece, Miss Jenna Winton."

"Jenna Winton." She forced her new name from her lips then stared out the window. On one side, the bush was thick and green, and on the other, the ocean was a deep crystalline blue and touched with the foam of white caps. No Tyler though. Not anywhere.

"Jenna, you should be aware that due to the circumstances of your open case, we're relocating you to Mr. Brown's high country station in Marlborough. His homestead will be your base, but not your confined lodgings. You will have the freedom of movement, provided you abide by the rules and regulations of the re-identification program, of which all points are fully outlined in your manual. Please be aware that with the remoteness of the station, Ronson has provided both employment and accommodations, and you should allow two to four weeks for initial settlement."

"Marlborough? Hold on. I'll be in the South Island of New Zealand?" Her heartbeat raced. They could have sent her anywhere in the world, but she would still be on home soil? Really? She scrambled to work out how many hours of travel Marlborough was from Saria in Auckland. It was still some distance since the Cook Strait flowed between the two islands, although less than a day's travel by road, even with the ferry crossing involved. Auckland was where Tyler would be too. So close, yet so far away.

"That's right, and Ronson is a man you can trust. So should you need to, you can converse with him as necessary. As ex-

Force, he can reach me at any time."

"Okay." She searched out the window, not wanting to miss the resort where Tyler should be as they flew overhead.

"You'll be his housekeeper and cook."

"Right." She could do that. "Are there any children?" She desperately hoped so. Children would help her settle.

"There's a station manager who lives on the property and he and his wife have two small children, but you're not responsible for them. There're also three eighteen-year-old boys who live on site in the staff barracks, but your duties again don't extend to them. As Ronson's niece, you'll live at the homestead, one which he's confirmed as a safe environment. You'll do well." He inclined his head toward her pack. "Open it. Try and make a start."

"What of Saria? Is she still with Ben?" She unzipped the pack and gripped the pages within.

"Of course. We're aware she wishes to go through re-identification as you have, but not until she sits her finals. We're happy to allow for this, and until then, Ben Hammers will guard her. Ben will continue his investigation into the newspaper leak and follow through on any other subsequent links. I'll take over your case from this point, but he'll remain on the issues he began with. He and I will work together to ensure a smooth transition for both you and your sister."

"Where will she go?"

"I can't disclose that information, only I can and will keep you apprised of her well-being as necessary. Why don't you familiarize yourself with your pack's information. This is a short flight to the mainland, and you should be prepared before we get there."

Again, she searched the island. There it was. The resort. She gripped her seat, but it was so far below, the people mere dots along the beach. Indistinguishable.

Closing her eyes, she stored the sight.

* * * *

At the resort's reception, Tyler signed for his long-awaited package. He raced past the indoor shops along the central walkway and to the beach. He had to get back. He'd already been gone too long.

He pulled his sunglasses from his top pocket and slid them on as he made the wharf. Within minutes, he'd powered away, his journey as swift as he could manage, except the cove's beach was deserted as he rounded the corner. Why? Everyone should still be there.

He sped toward the ship, pulled up to the side, roped the inflatable at the rear then climbed on board. In the lounge, Liam fidgeted on one of the couches while Nico cuddled into him. Luke rubbed Nico's back, and Dylan stood staring out the windows.

Brigs rose from a corner chair and raked a hand through his hair. "I've got bad news."

"Where is she?" Tyler's heartbeat thumped. He stepped toward Brigs, his fists clenched. She was gone. The knowledge raced like a firestorm through his blood.

Nico lifted his head and with reddened eyes cried, "Bad men. They took her."

His nephew's distress clawed at his gut, and he swung back to Brigs. "I was only gone a damn hour."

"Not bad men, but the extraction team." Brigs gritted his teeth. "You knew this would happen."

His heart dislodged, and the package in his hands fell and landed with a thunk on the ground. "She's alone, without me." And he had no way in hell of finding her.

"It was fast, but you know she chose this." Brigs held out a plastic bag containing her purple bikini and his white t-shirt.

He stared at it, his vision blurring, his mind shredding as every molecule in his body aggressively resisted the truth. He grabbed for air, his stomach heaving as a tidal wave of emotion rushed through him.

His mind filled with images, his blood on Lydia's hands as she clung to him, and another of bark on the trunk of an oak tree. It scraped into his hands as he gripped it. His back throbbed with each breath he dragged in. So much pain, and Lydia and Jay screaming from where he had them squished between him and the tree. He had to keep them safe.

He bundled her closer. "Shh, Brigs will come."

From across Lawntree's yard, Brigs shouted. Help was on the way.

His legs buckled and he fell to his knees. He dragged Lydia and Jay with him, and as he did, a man in camouflage gear slid over the high wooden-slatted fence and slunk away.

The threat to Lydia was gone.

"You stay with me, Tyler." She clasped his face, dragging his gaze back to hers. He stared into the eyes of an angel. "You're not going to die."

"No, not when I haven't yet kissed you." He wouldn't leave her, not like this, except his eyelids drooped, the weight too heavy to hold. "I-I." His heartbeat stuttered within his chest and the dark descended, taking her from him.

Chapter 10

Fingers pried at his right eyelid. He groaned, his mind slumping about within his head, and a piercing light flickered.

"Wake up, Mr. Whitehall. Your family is here and most anxious to see you. I'm Dr. Hardeef."

He shoved the doctor's hand away then rubbed his jaw and found a sharp growth of stubble. Why was he in a hospital?

The doctor's annoying voice droned on. "That's it. Open your eyes, sir."

Cranking his lids up, he stared at the man in the white coat, and jerked back as another beam of light hit his sensitive retinas. "Hey, I'm not blind."

"Uncle Tyler." His nephew scaled his metal-railed bed and bounced onto his chest.

"Oomph." Rolling onto his side, he slid Nico to the stiff hospital mattress, holding him close. Why were Nico's eyes all red and blotchy?

"We've been trying to wake you for a whole day." Nico clung to him.

"Um, maybe I was really tired." He frowned. No, that didn't sound right.

"You're in so much trouble with Daddy."

"He's in more than just trouble." Liam cut a path across the room, Dylan, Luke and Brigs storming in behind him.

The dark-skinned doctor backed away. "I'll return on my next round. It appears your family would like a word."

"Did someone slug me?" Tyler glanced upward as an oscillating fan pushed humid air down on him. "What am I doing here?"

"The answer starts and ends with one person." Brigs's jaw worked from side to side as he edged in front. "Do you remember why I came?"

"No."

Brigs planted his hands flat on his mattress. "You will be peeved at me if you don't remember. What's the last thing you recall?"

"Ah, weren't we at the cove?" There'd been a white sandy beach and Nico collecting shells with…

Brigs clicked his fingers in front of his face. "Come on. Get with the program." He turned and motioned to Luke. "Give Tyler the clothing."

Luke dumped a bundle in his hands. It was his white t-shirt, and…was that a purple bikini? "Yeah, thanks, but I prefer shorts." Still, he stared at the bikini, fingering the shiny fabric. "Is this supposed to mean something to me?"

"Okay, enough with the fooling around. Tell me who last wore this clothing, and make it snappy."

Examining the clothing, he brought the t-shirt to his nose and inhaled. Ah, the scent of the sea and the sand, and yes, just beneath was the trace of a woman's perfume. Damn, it smelt good. Like the sweetest white roses. Every cell in his body stirred to life.

He wanted, and with his senses on overload, he scrutinized his brothers. "Who the hell's worn my shirt?"

* * * *

"Jenna, is Colt back?" Nine days in at Ronson Brown's high country station and Lydia was just getting used to Ronson calling her new name.

She climbed the four raggedy steps to the wide wraparound porch of the homestead and dropped into the creaky wooden chair next to his. Flapping her Stetson in front of her face, she tried to cool down from her long walk. "I didn't see him at the feed sheds."

Ronson kicked his feet up on a wooden crate and rocked his chair back on its hind legs. Her new uncle might be ex-Force, but he was a young fifty-five, with only a sprinkling of gray at the sides of his dark hair.

"What did Marianne say?"

Colt's wife, the other half of the Australian couple who oversaw Ronson's station, Marianne, was so sweet. "After she cleaned up the boys, she said she'd radio him." The boys were wee Ethan and Eli, Marianne and Colt's adorable four-year-old twins. Those two scamps had stained their clothes and hands green sliding down the hill. Boy, Nico would've loved to have joined them in their fun. No. That couldn't happen. Her heart pulsed with pain.

Turning, she looked out over the rolling green hills that sloped down toward the beautiful Awatere Valley and the deep blue waters of the winding river nestled below. Nico's fifth birthday would come in a few days, which returned her thoughts with haunting force to Tyler. Her gut churned with how much she missed them all, Tyler's family and hers.

She sat forward and her glasses slid to the tip of her nose. "Ronson, these glasses truly suck." She shoved them back again.

He clasped his hands behind his head and stretched out even further. "The key for the truck is hanging in the mudroom on the hook by the door. Go and get them adjusted. You don't have to ask permission."

"I know. It's hard to get used to though." She surely loved heading into town. The hour-long drive and the freedom of traveling through the countryside eased the hurt in her heart. Ronson understood. "I'll go tomorrow. The shops will be closing soon and I won't get there in time if I leave now."

Blenheim, a town of thirty-thousand, sat at the top of the South Island. Perfectly remote, yet it still thrived with community.

"What am I cooking my favorite uncle for dinner?" She scuffed the soles of her leather boots against the dusty wooden deck.

He let out a chuckle. "Well, Jenna, until we can get you past burning everything, it all tastes the same. It's like you have no sense of smell."

"Usually I do." Although, when she tried to cook anything, she cried. When she cried, her nose stuffed up and she couldn't smell. "Saria loves to cook, and I love to eat what she makes. Cooking reminds me of all the times we shared."

"Jenna." Ronson's tone was soft. "Thoughts of your sister are good. Enjoy them, but don't get lost within them."

"I can't help it."

"You wanna talk? You know I have big ears. I understand you miss your sister and your family, just don't bottle it in."

She sucked in a breath. Ronson had a way of getting straight to the point. "I've spent months on end away from my family in the past, but never more than a few weeks from Saria. Usually I only have to pick up the phone and hear her—" Her heart ached with a depth that could barely be explained. "Then there's Tyler. He's gone from me in a way that feels like death."

"He's not dead." The crinkles around his eyes deepened as he frowned.

"I know, and Saria will always be my sister, but Tyler, well, he'll…move on."

"You love him?"

"I wish I could say no. It would make my life easier."

"Jenna, give yourself a break. Gilchrist said he's hard at work on your case. Keep the faith that one day Johnny Taita's killer will be found."

"It's been thirteen months. That's why I chose *this*."

"No. You chose *this* to protect your sister and the man you just told me you loved." He gently rubbed her arm. "One of the reasons I offered to provide sanctuary for you was because I took one look at your file and couldn't say no. I've told you Drake's story. He's six months out of juvie and doing incredibly well. We're a family here, and you're now our newest member. We look after our own."

She held onto his words, taking them deep into her heart. She could do this, still, no matter her new family on this station, her thoughts returned to Tyler. Always to him.

* * * *

Tyler's family had gawked, their expressions shattered as he'd stroked the purple bikini and white t-shirt bundled in his hands. Then all hell had broken loose as a razz of broken images flooded his mind from before he'd blacked out. He recalled his time on board The Idle Dream with Lydia, but more than that, the specific moment of the shooting a year past, small shards where he'd held onto Lydia and Jay before he'd slumped to the ground in a pool of his own blood. Hell, he remembered the shooting. Nothing more of the ten days he'd guarded her, but at least that fateful moment was back in his mind.

He'd told Brigs, and within minutes, he'd seen to his release. They'd boarded the ship and cut their holiday short, and returned across the Pacific to Auckland.

Nine days had passed, and he paced the confines of Ben's downtown city office. His need for Lydia stretched every nerve in his body to breaking point. He wrenched at the neck of his white button-down shirt. "I can't stand this."

"None of us can." Ben thrummed his fingers over the dark wood of his desk. "I've informed Gilchrist of your memory recall from the moment of the shooting. He knows you've got nothing more than that, but he's asked if you'll keep working with the in-house psychologist. You haven't told me how today's appointment with the doctor went."

"I got nothing more." He scrubbed his hands over his face. Lydia had once again been left with no choice but to battle through on her own. He should have been there when Gilchrist had come for her re-identification. He'd left her again.

"Tyler?"

With a low growl, he focused on Ben. "How's Saria doing with Lydia missing?" Ben had said he could take one of the shifts in guarding her, but she was Lydia's identical twin, and he wasn't sure he could see Saria and keep his head in the game.

"Lydia's not missing." Ben rose and crossed to the window. He leaned his shoulder against the wide sheet of high-rise glass. "She's somewhere safe and you need to remind yourself of that."

"I want her back."

"Yes, and to do that, we have to solve Johnny's case and find the killer."

Which he would. They all would. Ben and Brigs were both with him on this.

"Go." Ben pointed to the door. "You and Brigs have a lot of work to do. Sit with our systems specialist again. I want to know who leaked Lydia's details to the newspaper reporter. Go over every piece of information in those files. Find the killer."

It was all the incentive he needed. He was on it.

* * * *

Staring out the wide kitchen window to the valley below, Lydia scraped the blackened inside of a large pot.

"Throw it away, Jenna." Ronson came in behind her with a frown. "Okay, how did you burn the pot when all it held was potatoes?"

"I was distracted. My thoughts are rather annoying that way."

"Saria and Tyler?"

"Yeah." She set the pot down and reached for her ridiculously loose glasses from the windowsill. Yesterday

Ronson had said to get them repaired, which she would since they were part of her disguise. Her hair was a vibrant red, and she went nowhere without her glasses and Stetson. She was a country girl, and had to maintain the image.

"What ya thinking?"

"That I'm gonna go pick us up something to eat and bring it home. I'll deal with these glasses when I'm there." She slid them on her nose where they wobbled.

"Good idea, and make sure you grab a heap of those frozen dinners that get nuked in the microwave." He tugged up the waistband of his jeans. "I'm starting to lose weight. I didn't think that would happen with a new housekeeper and cook."

Feeling a touch bad, she squeezed his arm. "At least the homestead is spotless." She couldn't go wrong with her cleaning. She'd cleaned until her fingers were red and raw.

"Yep, I've surely never seen the place sparkle like this. Drive safe."

"Will do." She headed to the mudroom and snatched the truck's keys and her purse from the hook then high-tailed it out the back door.

Colt sauntered up from the yard, and he raised a hand. "Hey."

"Hey back at ya. How are the boys today?" She grabbed her glasses as they slid down her nose. Stupid disguise. She could handle the red hair, even though she still got the shock of her life each time she looked in the mirror. No one would recognize her now, not even her sister.

"Tearing around Marianne's feet, just where they usually are. I'm after Ronson. He inside?" Colt jumped the verandah steps two at a time as he joined her. The station manager was a big man with sun-darkened skin and scraggly blond hair poking out from under his Stetson.

"Yep, inside, and no doubt rummaging through the pantry for food." She groped for the handrail as she teetered down the steps.

"Thanks. Be careful there. You should get those glasses fixed. You're going to trip over your own two feet soon."

"I'll get on that right now. Catch ya later."

"Sure thing."

She reached the truck and tossed her oversized lenses to the passenger seat then started up her avenue to freedom. The dusty red truck rumbled to life, and she jerked on the wheel and drove down the gravel drive.

Turning onto the winding blacktop, she cranked the window open. A nice breeze fluttered the short sleeves of her tan half-button shirt, cooling her skin.

Relaxing into the drive, she let the good thoughts of Saria and Tyler prevail over all else. She would hold onto what she could, as Bronson kept telling her to.

The drive was long, but she made the corner gas station at the beginning of town within the hour. She eased out of the cab, wiped her faded blue jeans then unscrewed the lid on the tank.

"Hey, Red."

Drake. Only he called her red in honor of her bright locks.

He whistled low and long as he strolled over and leaned against her truck. Behind him, Slade and Tate, dressed in leathers as he was, filled their road-bikes.

Drake was one of Ronson's eighteen-year-old station hands. Drake acted tough, but she'd soon learnt he was a sweet-talking rascal. Slade and Tate lived with him in the barracks, just along from the feed sheds. "Have you boys got the afternoon off?"

"We surely do. Colt said we could go for a ride, but I'm hurt, Red. You said you'd take a spin with me the next time you left the station."

"I believe you left first."

"Maybe." He chewed his gum, his gaze sparkling. "But since we're in town, you could hop on the back of my bike now. Park the truck in the lot and we'll drive Main Street."

Slade and Tate cheered him on, and she winked at them. Slade was Colt's younger brother and visually his lookalike, while Tate was Slade's cousin. They were all family, and now hers too. "Next time, okay."

"I'll hold you to that." He grinned. "By the way, you look much hotter without those chunky glasses."

Oh no. She patted her eyes and found she'd left the damn things in the truck. "Ah, right. Could you fill the tank for me while I grab them?" She scrambled across the front seat and snatched them, his chuckles loud and clear as she did.

Setting her glasses in place, she peered at him while he refueled for her. "You're too smart for your own good."

"And you look sad. You like Ronson's place, don't you, Red?"

"I'm getting there." Like her, he had his own issues having spent six months in juvie. "What about you?"

"It's all good now." He ran his thumb over the nozzle while it filled. "I came from a crappy family, but this new one of Ronson's is the best."

"Really? Crappy?"

He looked at her and tipped up his chin. "Most of my dad's family is in the slammer, or just out, or just going back in. My mother and her family are in the money, but they don't know nothin' about me 'cause I'm a Hyena. I don't fit nowhere and never have. Ya get my drift?"

"I'm real sorry, Drake."

"Yeah, my mother shuffled me off as quick as she could to the old man. I was only a day old when she got me out of the way. I've only met her a handful of times, that's when she's had to come by and see Dad. But like I said, I'm in a good place now, and I'll make something of myself here."

"Ronson's definitely the best."

"His niece is hot too." He smiled mischievously.

"You're three years younger than me."

"I'll catch up."

"I don't think so, unless you can bend time."

His grin got wider. "We'll see." He finished pumping her gas and hung up the nozzle. "Take it easy. I won't forget I owe you a ride." He sauntered to his bike and revved it. "Later, Red."

She tossed him a wave as she headed to the counter and paid. That done, she started the truck and further along Main Street, parked outside the optometrist's.

Inside, she waited as the assistant adjusted her lenses and fit them nice and tight. Perfect, if one wanted glasses.

After leaving, she wandered to Gift-Giver, a novelty shop next door. With Nico's birthday so close, it was now or never if she wanted to send him something. Oooh, and right there on the center shelf, a gorgeous sandy patterned conch shell, one of the large varieties that when you blew in, made that distinctive island horn sound.

A saleslady joined her, a woman in a slim-line black skirt and white blouse. "I take it you like this?" she asked.

"Yes, although I thought it was illegal to remove these kinds of shells from the islands?" Nico had found one at the cove, but she'd said it had to stay.

"That's right, but this is a manufactured lookalike. They sound as good as the originals, and they are your only option if you're after a shell of this size."

"Then I'll take it." She handed it to her.

"Wonderful. Let me gift wrap it for you."

"Thanks. Do you courier as well?"

"We sure do. Come to the counter and fill out an address tag. What wrapping paper would you like?" She pointed toward a selection behind the counter.

Ahh, the perfect print sat in a roller at the top. "The blue one with the sailing ships. Thank you."

Nico would love it, only she wasn't allowed this kind of contact with anyone. But too bad. She'd send it to Gilchrist, and hope he'd pass it along, and if he didn't, well, at least she'd tried. It was the thought that counted, and right now, she needed that thought.

The saleslady smiled and wrapped the gift while she filled in the address tag. She passed it across, and the lady tied it to the winding ribbon she'd wrapped around it.

"When will it go?" She pulled out her new card to pay.

"The courier stops in at five. It'll be delivered late tomorrow."

"Perfect."

She left the shop with a bouncy step, and passed a red phone booth on the sidewalk. A man in scuffed black jeans and a green muscle tee crowded the small space. On his bicep was a large tat, one of a sharp-toothed hyena with a raised claw. She slowed, having seen that tat somewhere before. Hmm, but where?

"The brat was at the pumps," the man hissed into the phone. "He just drove down Main Street. No one ignores Kern, lady. About time you came through for me. I've been looking for your kid for six months." He slammed the phone into its cradle as he hung up, and the springy black cord tangled in on itself.

She ducked out of his way as he stormed past and glared at her.

Creepy.

Still, nothing and no one would alter her mood now.

Chapter 11

Staring out Ben's office window down Queen Street, Tyler gripped the sheet of paper Ben had handed him. "Can't you get me anything more than this?"

"I've retained very little in the way of access to Lydia's files. By the time Saria goes through re-identification, I'll have even less. I'm only working the angles you're following. You wanted to know about Lydia's wellbeing, and now you have your answer."

"All this tells me is she's made three calls to her handler since she went under. These calls do not tell me she's safe." Hell, he was exhausted, and going around in circles. He hadn't uncovered any further information. His disjointed memory of his shooting and the pain in her eyes haunted him. The image made him reach for her each night, but she wasn't there. She was gone, and he had to get her back.

"If she wasn't safe, I'd be the first one to tear into Gilchrist and demand access to her." Ben thumped his chest. "Saria asks about her too, and I have nothing to give either of you. I can't stand letting the girls down, yet I can't catch a break on this case. We have no motive for Johnny Taita's murder, and no evidence leading to who killed him. Lydia's eyewitness description is the only thing I have."

"I want her with me." He crushed and hurled the paper into

the bin.

"I get that, Tyler."

"Hey, a little less fighting in here." In chunky black boots, Brigs marched in. "Our systems specialist just nailed the ID login of the reporter who wrote about Lydia."

"About damn time." Tyler slapped his leg.

"Exactly. He finally hacked into the newspaper's computer network and accessed the hard drive, but he wasn't the only one. There's foreign code proving our reporter received the information about Lydia in a very irregular way. A hacker dropped the source information in for the reporter to read. Our guy believes he'll be able to narrow down and identify the hacker's routed IP address, but it'll take him a little time."

"Wow, the reporter's source is a hacker. They always protect their source." Tyler let out a low whistle. "The source must have a lot to lose if he needed to go further than normal media source protection."

"The hacker clearly wants to remain untraceable. This is a sensitive case, not to mention a very public one. Most of the people in this country have heard the Taita name."

"Keep on this, Brigs. I want everything we can get on this hacker." Ben tapped his watch. "I don't want to keep you two from making the appointment with the psychologist."

"Yeah, we need to go." Tyler had taken Brigs with him to each of his appointments. He'd feared he'd say something which wouldn't mean anything to him, but might pertain to Lydia's case. Brigs was his second set of eyes and ears having been the man he'd handed her over to for the initial rotation change. He made for the door, Brigs right behind him.

They passed through the internal office area, significantly quiet since it was the tail end of the day. As he passed his chair, he snatched his black leather jacket from the back of it and swung it over his shoulder. Outside the building, he hailed a taxi.

It was a short journey to the federal building, where security scanned and sent them through to reception. He waited in the queue, right behind a courier driver in his red and yellow uniform.

The man passed his deliveries across to the receptionist. "This boxed shipment is for Collins from Wellington, and the smaller wrapped package is for Gilchrist from Blenheim. Sign here."

She did, and the courier driver left with a brisk step.

Tyler nodded to the woman. "I've an appointment with Dr. Kevin Forsythe." He passed her his license, as did Brigs.

"One moment please." She checked her computer, tapping away on the keyboard. "Yes, take the elevator to the fourth floor. Room 403. The doctor is expecting you."

They rode the elevator up. The doctor's door was open and Tyler strode in. "Afternoon, Doc."

"Ah, Tyler, welcome back. Make yourself comfortable." He closed his laptop and rose from behind his solid walnut desk. "Brigs, anywhere you like, as usual."

"Thanks." Brigs closed the door, wandered to the window, and perched on the sill.

Tyler settled onto the long, green couch.

"How have you fared since we last spoke, Tyler?" The doctor picked up a pen and pad from the coffee table and sank into the armchair across from him. "And I'm referring to your dreams at night."

"They're nightmares, not dreams." Never-ending, or at least until he woke because he'd sweated out the sheets. "You said we'd work on storming my senses today. You were Lydia's assigned psychologist a year ago, so storm away."

"Right. We'll get straight to it then." He removed a micro recorder from his shirt pocket and set it on the coffee table. "Lydia may not have known Johnny Taita personally, but she saw the last moments of his life." The doctor looked over the rim of his glasses. "As she felt she did with you."

"I didn't die." He stared at doc's corner file cabinet, itching to peek inside Lydia's folder for anything to get closer to her.

"Lydia never saw you again, and she spoke of you in almost every session. She suffered over witnessing bullets meant for her striking you. I can't go into specific detail as that's client privilege, but I can say the reality of your near death was a heavy burden for her to carry. Particularly since she believed no one's life was worth more than another's simply because it was their job to protect."

"I left her when she needed me the most. I abandoned her, and that's how I see it." He examined the framed print of Rangitoto Island and the heavy bush which lined its sides, just like their cove.

"Tyler, you can't take upon yourself what you had no ability to control."

He stared at the man. "Doc, she's needs me now, and I'm still not there for her." His heart wrenched at the thought.

"No, but she's taken control of her own life by keeping those she's placed in harm's way safe. You have to see that."

"No, it's my job to keep her safe. It's my right."

The doctor tapped his pen on his pad. "Why is it your right?"

He grasped the recorder, wanting to make sure he'd hear his own words later. "Because I claimed her the moment she came back into my life. I'm living from one day to the next…for her. I can't give her the control she wants, not when my life is tied to hers."

"Leaving would have been a difficult decision. Lydia's an independent woman. You cannot control her."

Damn it. Tyler both adored her strength and despised it. "As I said, my life is tied to hers."

"Do you think she made the wrong choice?"

"Yes."

"Tyler, we have a problem. You keep laying the facts aside,

but the truth is the truth, no matter which way I present it."

"Hold on." Brigs vaulted to his feet then snapped his fingers as he paced around the armchairs. "Present it?" Brigs eyed Tyler. "The present for Gilchrist from Blenheim. Sorry, Doc, but Tyler when is Nico's birthday? The wrapping paper had sail boats on it, like for a child."

"A couple of days." Hell, who on earth would send Gilchrist a package like that, except Lydia? This was either the breakthrough he'd waited for, or a desperate stab in the dark.

Regardless, he was on his feet. "Whatever was just said in this office, Doc." He squeezed the device as he raced for the door. "Remains between us."

At the elevator, he punched in the button for the ground floor.

Brigs heaved in a breath as he chased him. "Ben told me if the opportunity arose, to help you find her, not that Gilchrist can know."

Tyler slapped his shoulder. "Great. I appreciate the support, more than you can know. And this gift better be from her. She could be anywhere in the world, but Blenheim?" Yeah, if she was there, she'd been placed close.

The doors opened on the lower floor and he was off. Only one place in the world called his name, and if his woman was there, he'd find her. He wouldn't accept any other outcome.

* * * *

"Hey, it's Red." Drake leapt up the porch steps and bumped into Lydia where she leaned against the waist-high railing trying to swallow down a late lunch. She'd made a sandwich, but it was the most unappetizing one on the planet. "You look a bit green around the cheeks, Red."

"The gills," she mumbled around her mouthful, and then spat it back onto her plate. "Yuck. I want to be sick." She set her plate down on the steps. "Okay, so it's your turn to check on me, huh?"

Ronson had gone down country for the day to the cattle sale yards and had left her on her own for the first time. He'd been a touch worried, and told everyone to visit her in turns. He took the whole family thing right to heart, not that she minded. She could use the company.

"Yeah, but I also had to come back to grab a rifle from the locked cupboard in the mudroom."

"What's happened? Why do you need a gun?" Her heartbeat raced.

"One of the yearlings tried to cut across the river at the low point and went down. The poor thing got tangled in the bushes on the edge. Colt and me heaved her out, but the girl's leg is twisted and likely broke. The vet's been called, but Colt wants the gun. She's in pain." He rubbed his arms, rucking up his short sleeves. As he did, his bicep tattoo, one of a hyena peeked out.

She tugged the sleeve higher, exposing the hyena's sharp-toothed snarl. Ah, this was where she'd seen that tattoo. "What does this mean?"

Turning his arm to the side, he eyed it. "My last name's Hyena and this is a family tat, only one I don't care to associate with since I'm better off without them. I told you I had a crappy family. My dad, who's an ugly son of a coot and actually looks like a hyena by the way, thought he'd take me to the Tat Club on my sixteenth. That's where I had this ink done. But this is no gift. This is a mark from hell." He dug in his pocket and drew out a cigarette and lighter.

"Nice family."

"Yep. Why'd ya ask what the tat meant?" He shoved the unlit cigarette between his lips.

"I saw a man downtown yesterday with one, or almost the same one, right after we were at the gas station. His hyena had a raised claw though, but other than that they're alike."

"Dad's tat doesn't have a raised claw, but my uncle's does." His gaze narrowed as he lit his cigarette and took a deep drag until the tip glowed red and hot. "You stay away from Ladd if you see him. He's the worst, as bad as Dad. I ended up in juvie because of both of them."

"What happened?"

"It was right after I'd had this ink done at Wellington's Tat Club. My dad and Ladd took me with them to what should have been a business meeting, only it was anything but. The back alley at the club was dark and I was told to wait outside while they disappeared inside. A few minutes later gunshots rang out and a window broke over my head. When I looked up, a body came at me at warp speed from three floors up. I ducked but the dead dude landed on top of me and broke one of my legs. I blacked out, and after I came to, the boys in blue were there. Dad and Ladd had dumped me and left."

"I'm so sorry."

He snorted. "It's fine. I was used to the cloak and dagger stuff. After the doctors fixed me up, I was tossed into juvie until Ronson came along and organized counsel to clear me. Ronson was retiring, and my case was the last one to cross his desk. He took an interest in me when no one else did."

"Why didn't they go to jail?" Clearly his uncle wasn't in the slammer since she'd seen him.

"Neither of them did. I've been told they had alibis for the night, and they said I was just a stupid kid. I didn't even see who made the shot, so nothin' I said counted." His tone was bitter, and she totally understood why. Crappy was not a strong enough word for his family.

She squeezed his arm. "You've left your past behind. You should be proud of where you're at now."

"Yeah, and everyone here is my family, only I don't like that you've seen Ladd. He's got no business being in Blenheim."

Chills raced down her spine. "Ah, I overheard him on a pay phone saying he'd seen the brat at the pumps, and no one ignores Kern. He called her lady, told her it was about time she came through for him, that he'd been searching for her kid for six months. I think I got that right. Does any of that make sense?"

Puffing on his cigarette, he slanted his head. "Kern is my father. He came to me in juvie, saying he was sick. He looked it too, something about kidney failure. He wanted one of mine, and I got tested. I was a match, but I was never gonna give it to him. It was just sweet to have something over him for a change."

"So, the lady would be your mother?"

"My stuck-up mother's never wanted me on the scene, abandoned me at birth. She married a white collar, like she is. I've only ever seen her a handful of times, when Dad had her come by, but if anyone could find me here, she could. She's into computers and all."

"Why would your mother help your dad and Ladd try to find you?"

His mouth turned down. "Dad's got something over her. He always did since I'm her dirty little secret. He makes her do stuff, you know with the computer when he needs it. I stay out of the way."

"I still don't feel right about any of this. You should talk to Colt since Ronson's away and let him know what's going on. Your uncle sounded like he meant business. He did say he'd already seen you by the pumps."

That had to have been when Drake had filled her tank up, maybe ten minutes before she'd seen his uncle at the phone booth. She shivered. Yuck.

"I guess I was watching you too much. Still, I got nothin' to fear anyway, not when I got a kidney Dad wants. Ladd does what Dad says. There's a pecking order in my family, if ya get my meaning."

"Hey, Drake."

Slade jogged around the corner, holding his Stetson on his head with one hand.

"Yo, here."

"Bro." Slade came to a stop in front of them. "You've taken so long. Colt needs that rifle down at the crossing." He flapped a hand through the air, dispersing Drake's cigarette smoke. "And you've gotta stop smoking. Marianne will throw a fit if she sees you doing that anywhere near her kids. Get a hurry on. We have work to do."

Drake grinned and leaned a hand against the wide rail "Red here was lonely and whistled out for a little company."

Smart Drake was back in full form.

Slade rolled his eyes and turned back the way he'd come. "Come on, get your butt moving. I'll grab the gun."

Drake plucked the cigarette from his mouth and dropped the butt to the porch, and then used the heel of his boot to extinguish it. "Later, Red. It seems they can't work without me around here."

She liked Drake. He was a good kid, and second chances counted, something he'd been given, and so had she. Yeah, she was already indebted to Ronson for all he'd done for her, but now she had an even greater appreciation of the man who was ex-Force. In her eyes, he was a hero for taking on a kid who needed to escape his own family.

With the boys gone, she walked inside and set her plate on the kitchen counter. She strolled into the living room and navigated around the couches.

She tugged up her jeans at the knees, knelt and reached for yesterday's newspaper Ronson had tossed between his favorite recliner and the coffee table. Crumbs from his sandwich slid off the paper and onto the floor. Drat.

After she dropped the paper onto the stack at the back door, she opened the hall cupboard and rummaged inside for the vacuum cleaner. She hauled the artifact out, unraveled the cord then plugged it into the living room's mains.

She flicked the switch and the motor rumbled to life, only the rumble whirred quickly into a high-pitched squeal. She clamped her hands to her ears as the motor shrieked. Black dust billowed from the back of the machine along with a snakelike hiss.

Not good. At all.

She dived for the power switch, snapped it off and heaved the cord free. Air. She needed fresh air. With a hand over her mouth, she stumbled and ran for the back door.

On the porch, she sucked in long drafts of air. "Now, that would be just my—"

A gunshot blasted somewhere down in the valley, and she jerked upright.

Her heart bumped out of rhythm, the shot drumming in her ears, pounding against her temples. She lifted her hands and Tyler's blood coated them, dripping from her fingers, pooling on the ground.

"No!" It was just an illusion, and she shook her head, so hard her teeth rattled.

This wasn't real. There was no blood. The cow had been shot. That was all.

She slammed her eyelids shut.

"Get it together. Tyler's safe." Sweat trickled down her back. She had to get out of here and find somewhere else to breathe, even if only for a little while. Town. Even the long drive would help. It always did.

She snatched the keys from the mudroom and jumped into the truck. She clawed the steering wheel as she revved the engine and busted down the drive.

Tyler. She was here for him and for Saria, to make sure she never placed either of their lives in danger again, and by the time she made it into town, that mantra had gone through her head and was once again set firm.

She wiped her forehead as she pulled into the parking lot in front of the Mega Store. Removing her glasses with one hand, she squeezed the bridge of her nose with the other. She could do this. She was strong.

Plunking the glasses back on, she stared at the store in front of her. Yeah, life moved on, and it seemed she had a new vacuum cleaner to buy.

* * * *

Tyler had driven overnight down country to Wellington with Brigs in the passenger seat, and they'd boarded the morning ferry across the Cook Strait to the South Island. From there, Blenheim had been a short drive. He surveyed the length and breadth of Blenheim's Main Street from where he'd parked the SUV.

The town was home to thirty-thousand, and he had the job of finding one small woman, and no solid place to start. No, that wasn't right.

He frowned at Brigs who rested his butt on the front grill. "Can you believe we've come all this way, and we're going to start looking for wrapping paper?"

"With sailing boats, mate." Brigs grinned. "Such is the life of a bodyguard. I never would have guessed I'd have signed up for this."

"Huh. I'd laugh, but that's just not funny." He was desperate to get Lydia back. He wanted her with him. And for her to reach out and send Nico a gift meant she was hurting. That was something he couldn't allow.

"We'll find her."

"We better."

"Then let's get ourselves into gear." Brig's pushed off the front grill and slapped dust from his wrinkled pants. "First we need clothes and supplies since neither of us took the time to pack anything."

Keeping a lookout, Tyler set out along the pavement. "I don't care about clothes. What do you think she'll look like?" Surely he'd know her, no matter any disguise she'd been given.

"It's anyone's guess. Gilchrist would've had her completely

made over." Brigs pointed to the Mega Store. "That place has everything, including clothes and wrapping paper. We'll need a suitcase too."

"If we find the same paper stocked here, we'll request video surveillance and go through it." Eager to move on this, he strode through the parking lot. Automatic doors swished open for him, and for every reason, he couldn't enter fast enough.

* * * *

Crouching in front of the vacuum cleaners, Lydia ran her hand over a compact model she could easily carry upstairs and maneuver around the rooms.

Perfect, and only two-hundred and ninety nine.

She heaved it from the shelf and set it into her trolley.

She dusted off her hands and adjusted her Stetson.

She froze.

No way! She swore under her breath.

She whipped off her glasses and scrubbed her eyes. Two very familiar looking men had just passed her aisle.

Im-poss-i-ble.

Jamming her glasses back on, she focused. It wasn't as if they'd be in her neck of the woods by chance. Nooo. Tyler and Brigs had tracked her down. She scooped up her long hair and shoved it underneath the brim of her Stetson.

She tiptoed to the end of the aisle then peeked around the corner.

Oh boy. Tyler wore a pair of black pants low on his hips, his blue dress shirt crumpled as if he'd slept in it. He turned down the far aisle at the end of the store.

She shrunk back against the shelves. A mountain of thoughts dumped into her mind making her dizzy. She'd gone through re-identification to keep him safe, yet still he'd found her. Well, almost found her. Heck, if he'd found her, could the killer too?

Adrenaline surged through her veins and her stomach

rolled. Fear for his safety shot through her. Only a heartbeat later, her desperate need to see him overruled. She wanted to step out of hiding and go to him.

Tyler was here, and more than anything in the world, she had to see him.

Before she knew it, she was at the end of the luggage aisle. Ahead, he snagged a case from the top shelf. His midnight black hair curled around his nape and onto his shoulders, an inch longer and still not cut. Sweet heaven, he looked gorgeous.

She glanced in either direction, but no one was nearby.

Tyler passed the case to Brigs.

"Tyler." His name shot from her mouth.

He rocked on his heels. "Brigs, tell me I didn't just hear my name."

"Shoot, you did."

Tyler whipped around and faced her. "Hell, Lee?" He stumbled toward her, his eyes rolled until the whites showed, then he slithered to the floor and landed in a heap at her feet.

Okay, that was not quite the welcome she'd expected.

Brigs stared at her. "I'd swear right now, but I'm too happy to see you." He knelt and pressed a finger to Tyler's pulse. "Mate, this is really the wrong time to flameout again." Brigs grabbed her hand and tugged her down beside him. "And you, don't move."

Chapter 12

"Tyler, wake up." Brigs propped him against the shelves and slapped both his cheeks. "Nope, he's completely out of it, Lydia. We're lucky we're in the back corner."

She crawled between Tyler's splayed legs. "You said again. How many flameouts has he had before this?"

"Last time was after you left. We had to wait it out at the hospital on the main island. It took him twenty-four hours to come around."

"Twenty-four hours?"

"Yeah. After he woke, it was with fragmented pieces of memory, but only from the moment he got shot. That's the one memory which came back."

"I didn't know. Was he in any pain?" Why hadn't Gilchrist told her about this when they'd spoken? "He didn't recall anything new?"

"No."

She took Tyler's hands lying limp at his sides and rubbed them between her own. "C'mon, sleepyhead. Open your eyes for me. I can't wait twenty-four hours to see you again. It's been weeks."

Brigs cleared his throat. "Keep talking to him. I'll go keep a lookout and make sure no one comes down here. You've gotta wake him up."

She leaned in and touched her nose to Tyler's. "I can't believe you're here. I also can't believe you're out of it." No answer, so she touched her lips to his. "I'm sorry about the way I left you."

Still nothing, not even a flicker of movement.

She nibbled at his ear. "I am going to ravish you in the middle of this aisle, and this is your last warning before I do."

His legs twitched and he groaned. "Lee?"

"About time." She smiled as he rubbed his eyes and looked at her. "It was the word ravish, wasn't it? I'll have to use that more often."

"That and the fact I don't have time to lie about when you have a habit of disappearing before I know it." He gripped her around the waist. "My head's a little fuzzy with new images, but ravish away."

"New images? You mean even more?"

He knocked off her hat and her hair rippled down, swaying to her bottom. "Damn, the red's beautiful." His lips lifted and he removed the wide-rimmed black spectacles from her nose. "After my first flameout I recalled the shooting. Not the most pleasant of memories, but along with it came the emotion I'd felt. We were close right at that time, and I finally had that memory back. Now I have everything, if I can just sort it."

"You mean everything, everything?"

"There's a scramble of new images, but I'll get there." He pushed his hands into her hair and stroked her scalp. "I know our circumstances are difficult, but I'll always be with you, no matter where you are."

Her heart flipped in her chest. "You said that to me in Wellington, a year ago."

"I know. I remember, now."

Brigs whistled. "Guys, mother with two kids approaching."

Tyler moved in a flash. One second she'd been between his legs on the floor, the next on her feet and tucked in behind him.

He pressed her hat and glasses into her hands. "Put them on."

She set them in place, managing it just as two little girls, one dressed in a pink t-shirt and shorts, the other in a white baby-doll dress, darted around the corner and into their aisle. The girls' brown ponytails bobbed as they ran, and their mother chased them, calling for them to slow.

Brigs came in beside them as the children and their mother continued on. "Okay, good to see you're up. Did I hear you right from down there? You have more recall?"

"Yeah, but it's still a jumble."

Brigs slowly smiled. "Ahh, at least your flameouts were worth it."

"Every single second of them." Tyler slid his hand into hers then swung her around in front of him. "In the meantime, I need a name. Yours."

She rose up onto her toes and kissed him. "It's Jenna Winton. Nice to meet you."

"Where do you live?"

"On a high country station about an hour from here. I came into town to pick up a new vacuum cleaner for the one that just bombed. Ronson Brown is my uncle and he's ex-Force. Now, can we get back to the ravishing?"

"Have you bought it yet?"

"The vacuum cleaner?"

"Yes."

"It's in a trolley, a couple of aisles over. I saw you and left it behind. Ravishing, remember? I should get something for all that information I shouldn't have just given you."

"We're in a public place, Lee. I can't draw any undue attention to you, no matter you now have the freedom to move around."

"It's Jenna." She glanced at the cases on the floor. "Are you here to stay?"

"Only to find you. Let's get your trolley."

"You know, I remember when you were more fun." She winked at him over her shoulder as she sashayed toward her forgotten trolley.

"I remember that time too. Watch where you're walking."

"You're still bossy." She pushed her trolley into the main aisle toward the checkouts. Wow, she'd gone through re-identification, and still, he'd tracked her down. Although, what happened now?

* * * *

Tyler followed Lydia through the store. Her hips swayed far too enticingly. "Brigs, get her to slow down." If he did, he'd stop her completely.

Brigs moved ahead and gripped Lydia's shoulder. "We came with nothing, Jenna. Do you mind waiting while we grab some things?"

Jenna. Tyler had to remember to call her Jenna. Damn, he needed to be alone with her, and soon.

"Sure." She grinned at Brigs, then turned and lowered her lashes at him. "The men's department's this way. Come along, boys."

His gut burned to drag her to his side and make sure she never left him again. Instead he had to keep his hands off her and somehow follow as she weaved through the store.

Brigs knocked his shoulder with his hand. "It was a lucky break finding her, but I need to make a call to Ben and update him."

"You do that, and tell him once my mind clears and things slot back into place, I'll send him a report." Tyler removed a black Stetson from a hook and set it on his head. The fit was good, and he needed to blend in with the locals if she lived in the high country.

"Remember she has to stay here, and Gilchrist can never know we found her."

"Gotcha." Gritting his teeth, he turned back to Lydia. She

129

pulled jeans and t-shirts off a rack and slung them over her arm.

"I'll catch up with you two outside." Brigs took off as Lydia crossed to him.

"Where's he going?" She passed him her bundle.

"Somewhere quiet where he can't be overheard. He's calling Ben." He tucked the clothing she'd given him under one arm. "I need toiletries too."

"So, you're staying for how long?" Her luscious lips lifted in a smile.

"Not nearly long enough." He pressed her back into a gap between the men's jackets and sweaters. "A day or two, but Brigs and I'll lay low so we don't blow your cover."

"That'll be strange with you hiding out for a change." She ducked under his arm with the cheekiest grin. "Toiletries. This way."

He followed her from the clothing department to a series of shorter aisles. She slowed before the men's razors and picked through the selection until she found the same brand he'd used on the ship. A couple of steps along, she nabbed a toothbrush and a box of condoms and dropped them into his hands.

His arms bulged with his purchases and the condoms stared him hard in the eye. "Now I need a bed. With you in it."

She giggled and reached for her trolley. "Well, we agree on that. I'll go put this vacuum cleaner on Ronson's account and meet you in the parking lot."

"Sure, but stay where I can see you." The thought of her being out of his sight, even for a moment, ate a hole in his gut. How he'd leave her in a couple of days, he had no idea. It wasn't something he even wanted to contemplate.

* * * *

At the truck, Lydia opened the passenger door and heaved the box in. Brushing her hands together, she shut the door with her hip. Tyler was inside at the counter paying for his purchases, his gaze locked on hers through the wide storefront windows.

Behind her a bike rumbled and she turned as Slade rode into the parking lot. She jogged over to him, smiling wide. "Hey, Slade. What are you doing in town? Got another afternoon off?"

With one booted foot on the blacktop, he flipped the visor of his helmet and darted a look toward the truck. "Colt said to find you and bring you to the hospital. There's been an accident at the station. A bad one."

"What?" She grabbed his arm. "Is anyone hurt?"

He took her Stetson and jammed it into the bag tied at the back of his bike. He snatched the spare helmet, and slid it over her head. "I'll tell you on the ride. Jump on. This can't wait."

"What kind of accident?"

"There's no easy way to tell you this, but Drake's been shot. The rescue chopper flew him straight to the hospital." He pulled her on.

Hearing the word shot had her heartbeat hammering. "H-how b-bad?"

"It was intentional. Colt called Ronson, and he's on his way."

"Get a move on." Bunching her hands into the back of his shirt, she jerked him to hurry. If Drake was in the hospital, then that's where she needed to be.

Squealing out of the lot, Slade left a drag of rubber. She held on tight as she yelled into the rush of wind. "How'd all this happen?"

"We were at the river. Colt was ready to put the animal down and his shot and another from back within the trees went off. We didn't see who fired it, but it was a dirty shot and hit Drake right in the back."

Shot in the back, just like Tyler. No correlation, but every correlation. Her breath seized in her lungs as they sped through the streets. Black and gray swirled into one, the dirty color tinted with the murderous shade of blood red. Images flashed through her mind, of Johnny Taita's mangled body on the pavement, of

Tyler's blood on her hands. Why Drake?

Frustration welled and her anger soared. This had to end.

From behind, an almighty roar from a black SUV with darkened glass bore down on them. Tyler had his head half out the window as he drove, and Brigs gestured with his hand out the passenger's side for them to stop.

"We'll be there in a minute," Slade shouted to her.

Clasping her knees tightly to Slade from behind, she tucked in against his back. Hopefully Tyler would see she trusted whoever she rode with.

They peeled through the hospital's opened gates, following the curved drive to the entrance where a series of multi-story buildings stood. Slade pulled into a space before the main doors as a screech of tires and car doors opening heralded Tyler's arrival.

He lifted her clear of the back of the bike, his dark hair a disheveled mess. His gaze burned with fury. "What the hell's going on?"

Brigs gripped Slade by the lapels of his jacket and hauled him from his bike.

"No, Brigs. Slade was told to bring me here. Let him go."

Towering over him, he eyed the boy. "Kid, you better have one damn good reason for driving at that speed with Jenna on the back."

"Who are you?" Slade's gaze jumped from Brigs to Tyler. "Cops?"

"Friends of Jenna's," Brig's answered as Tyler backed her up.

"Let Brigs deal with this," Tyler muttered in her ear.

On the tips of her toes, she tried to see over his broad shoulders. "Slade said Drake was shot at the station, and Colt told Slade to come get me. Ronson's on his way."

"Someone got shot? That you know?"

"Yes." She swayed on her feet and bumped noses with him.

"Tyler—" So woozy.

"You've gone ghostly white. Are you okay?" He captured her close.

"I don't feel so good." Her vision blurred. "But I need to see Drake and make sure he's okay."

"No, you need to sit and catch your breath. If this Drake is in the hospital, he'll be in the best of care. You though, are mine to look after. Brigs," he yelled. "You go with that boy. I'll watch…Jenna."

"I've got my cell. Keep yours on hand." Brigs walked off with Slade.

"Are you sure I can't—"

"Yes. Get in." He opened the door and with no choice, she slid into the front seat of his SUV.

"Where are you taking me?"

"Not far." He reversed and drove to the far side of the parking lot, into a space where a curved garden of thick green bushes with white flowers hid them completely from view.

He turned the engine off then yanked her into his lap. "Just relax, okay?"

"I can't believe Drake got shot. Slade said it was down by the river. A dirty shot in the back."

"Hell, this just gets worse." He jammed his fist over the door locks and shoved them home. Tucking her cheek to his chest with one hand, he flipped open the glove compartment and withdrew his gun. He set it on the dash.

"The shooting had nothing to do with me. You don't need that."

"It's instinct to have it on hand where you're involved. Ignore it's there." He lifted the lever on his seat and pushed them back.

"I'm sorry I left with Slade the way I did. I don't know why this happened to Drake."

"Brigs will find out. You're safe, and that's all that matters.

It's best you wait it out here with me, until we get more clarity on this."

"Thank you for coming." She ran her hands over his chest and around to his back, driven by old memories to make sure he wasn't bleeding. "Sorry, I had a bit of a flashback on the ride."

"I'm in one piece."

Eyes closed, she snuck her nose into the low v of his blue shirt. He was solid and strong, and with her. "I know this isn't the right time, but…" She pulled the ends of his shirt free, hoping he understood what she needed.

"Are you sure? You're in shock." He halted her hands.

"I'm more than sure. No one can see through the tinted windows, right?"

He didn't answer her with words, but with actions, unzipping and dragging her jeans down, taking her pink panties with them. As he rolled her underneath him, he slid her red cotton tank top over her head.

"If you want to stop, tell me." Leaning in, he nuzzled into her bra.

"Never." She rubbed against him, moaning as he took one nipple deep into his mouth and sucked. He stayed there, covering her other breast with his hand and caressing.

He was so overdressed. She lowered his fly and released his cock.

Oh yeah. Much better. Now she had more of what she wanted.

With a moan he cupped her bare bottom and nudged her legs wider. "I missed you. Bad." He slid his finger along her entrance, playing with her clit.

She gasped and bucked against his hand, arching her back. "Show me."

He took her mouth in a long kiss as he pushed a second finger in and stroked with tortuous perfection. Sublime. "Like you wouldn't believe."

Gripping his shirtfront, she rode his hand, somewhere in the process of it all, feeling the change from wicked fingers to thick heavy cock.

"Tyler." He filled her up as he rocked into her. It was so right the way he joined with her.

"Let go, Lee. I'm right here with you." Then with the skill of his mouth taking hers, she flew, his body driving her hard over the edge and into complete oblivion.

Chapter 13

Lydia's lids fluttered open. Mmm, Tyler's body was hot over hers, and she didn't care that she couldn't move, not after the orgasm long denied her.

"Wow." She found her breath as his cock twitched deep inside her channel. "It looks like you're ready for round two." Once was never enough, not for either of them.

He tucked a length of hair behind her ear as he rolled to his side. "I would, but my cell phone's vibrating. It'll be Brigs." He lugged it out of his pocket.

She licked her lips. What a gorgeous body he had, or at least what was exposed to her eager eyes.

"I can't answer it if you're looking at me like that." With a grin, he adjusted his pants and zipped them up. "Hey, Brigs."

Edging closer, she angled her ear to hear. "Tyler, it's safe to come in. The boy Drake Hyena is out of surgery. They've removed the bullet and the doctor's just told everyone he'll make a full recovery. Jenna's new family is asking where she is."

"Thanks. We'll head in now." He pocketed his cell then let out a ragged sigh. Slowly, he drew her panties and jeans into place. "I never have enough time with you. That really has to change."

"I agree." She shuffled and clipped her bra on. Oh, it was so tight, her breasts far fuller than normal.

"Do you need a hand?"

"Yeah, where'd you throw my shirt this time?"

"I hardly call this a shirt." He fetched her tank top from the back seat and slid it over her head.

"I need to use the bathroom."

"Changing the subject, are you?" He switched the door locks off and hopped out. After reaching back in, he pulled her to her feet.

"Oh, my glasses." She retrieved them and slid them onto her nose.

He tucked her under his shoulder and walked her to the entrance.

"I won't be long." She veered toward the restrooms and shoved open the heavy swinging door. In front of the mirror, she stared at her reflection. Ugh. Her hair was so knotted. She marched to the large metal dispenser on the wall. Hopefully it held the usual things a woman needed.

Yep, there were pads, tampons, test kits and ah, combs. Perfect.

Whoa. Pregnancy test kits?

Leaning her hands flat against the dispenser, she dragged in a deep, deep breath. Okay, she was after a comb, not a test kit, except the only thought racing through her head was the fact she hadn't had a period since she'd boarded Tyler's ship. She should have had one by now, like over a week ago.

Sure, this past week she'd been unable to eat and felt sick when she did. Her breasts were bigger, and she'd never been on the pill. Heck. They hadn't used protection that first night or much in the first few days, and yeah, right then in the SUV. Tyler's use of condoms wasn't that great.

Oh boy.

After slipping a ten-dollar note into the dispenser, she selected the test kit. The machine shuffled one forward and dropped it out.

Oh boy. Oh boy.

She dragged her feet to the bathroom stall. Then following the instructions, she waited the mandatory one minute with her head bent between her knees.

How could she have let this happen? She was in The Program.

Her watch beeped, but she already knew the answer. The truth resonated deep in her heart.

As she lifted her head, she ran her finger over the tiny red symbol, and it was positive, without a doubt.

Crap.

* * * *

Tyler rapped his watch as everyone who'd gone in after Lydia left, and still, no sign of her. What could be taking her so long?

Finally the door swung open and she emerged. With his mind so strained with need, he almost barreled her down as he grabbed her. Something was wrong. Her face was flushed, her hair still a tumbled mess. Cupping her cheeks in his hands, he looked into her eyes. "What's wrong?"

"I-I—" She drew in a shaky breath. "There was a dispenser with test kits."

He had no idea what a test kit was, but a test of any sort didn't sound good going by her current reaction. Then she passed him a little white stick, and a red plus sign pulsed at him like a stoplight at an intersection. "Ah, is this what I think it is? A pregnancy test?"

"Yes." Her single word was filled with such anguish. Tears flowed down her cheeks. "I'm sorry. This wasn't even on my radar until I went in there."

She was pregnant. Lydia was going to give him a son or a daughter and Nico a cousin. He slid the small life-changing stick into his pocket and clutched her close.

Damn. Now he had a woman deep in The Program and an

unborn child to protect, a difficult task considering he struggled to stay in control of his emotions around her, and wasn't even supposed to be here.

"Tyler." Brigs jogged toward them, skirting people strolling the main corridor.

He turned back to Lydia and gently wiped her tears away. "We'll talk about this later."

She hiccupped. "Y-you—"

"Guys." Brigs stepped up to them. "You two took so long, I thought I'd better come." He eyed Lydia. "Hey, I know you've had a rough day, but the kid is fine."

"Let's go." Tyler wrapped an arm around her waist and guided her down the corridor. They passed a cafeteria bustling with doctors and nurses then slowed as they neared the elevators.

Brigs edged in closer as people passed by. "You should know Colt and his wife and kids, along with biker-boy, Slade, and another young boy named Tate, are all up there. Colt spoke to Ronson Brown earlier on the phone and he's on his way. He should be here within the half hour."

"This is getting complicated." The metal doors swished open and the three of them stepped inside. Tyler jabbed the close button before anyone else could join them. Lydia was the one woman in the world he'd never turn his back on. The stick in his pocket only cemented that decision. "Ronson Brown will need to know who I am."

Lydia's gaze darted to his. "What? No. I can accept your visits in secret, but Gilchrist will have me moved if he finds out I broke the rules and had contact with you. You can't tell Ronson. He'll tell Gilchrist."

"I can't look after you the way I need to from a distance. Not now." He squeezed her hands.

"Yes, you can. Nothing's changed. I mean, apart from the stick."

Brigs moved toward the control panel and halted the

elevator. "Okay, guys. What's the stick?" And must I point out we can't jeopardize Jenna's re-identification, Tyler. The occasional visit on the down low will work, but speaking to Ronson won't. He's ex-Force. He'll contact Gilchrist."

"Lydia's pregnant."

Brigs's eyes popped open at his abrupt comment, and then narrowed to slits. "That is not even remotely funny. She's in The Program."

"I realize that, which means if I must, I'll go under with her."

"You'd have to give up your family. Think, Tyler. Your brothers wouldn't deal with that, and Nico's only four."

Lydia shoved him away. "You are not giving up your family and your job and your friends for me. Not when you can hide out when you come."

"I'm staying with you, and you don't have a choice in the matter."

"No. You. Aren't." Her glower was fierce, a firm reminder the woman he dealt with was strong. She had left him once before, and he shouldn't forget.

"I'm staying."

"Not a chance."

"We're having a baby, and you're going to have to deal with the decision I've made."

She dropped her head into her opened palms. "I am going to explode, or at the very least my head is."

He pulled her into his arms. "I'll talk to Ronson and see if he'll accept my presence without informing Gilchrist, but I don't hold out much hope on that. Those who work for the Force are rigid in keeping to the rules."

"Right now, I really I hate you."

"But you understand?"

"I understand I hate you."

Hell, she had his heart in her hands. "You'll come around,

Lee."

Brigs snorted. "I don't know whether to congratulate you both, or bang your heads together."

"The banging of heads would be best," she mumbled against his chest.

Tyler chuckled, shocked to find her words actually soothed him, or it could be that she was burrowing closer, sliding her arms around his waist and gripping him. "Okay, do you have any idea why Drake was shot?"

"No."

Brigs hit the release button on the stalled elevator. "Let's get upstairs and start asking some questions. We need more than a no."

"Are there any police up there?" Lydia whirled and faced Brigs.

"A detective's on his way."

The doors opened on the surgical ward, depositing them right outside the waiting room. Two small children cried, one a boy with sandy blond hair who sat in the arms of his mother, the other an identical child who clung to his father. The children's sobs wrenched at his heart.

Lydia gasped and dashed past him toward the father who held one of the boys. The man must be Colt.

"Jenna." He jumped to his feet, holding out a hand to her. "I've been so worried. Ronson said I had to keep an eye on you, so I sent Slade to track you down." Colt glanced at Brigs then him as they followed her. "Brigs there told me you'd met him and his friend in town, and when they saw you on the back of Slade's bike, they thought they'd make sure you were okay."

"That's right." She stroked the child's back he held. "Colt, this is Tyler. I was a bit upset and he stayed with me until I calmed. Sorry to take so long."

"You look all right now, and that's what counts." Colt extended his hand to Tyler. "Thanks for looking after Jenna."

"No problem." Tyler shook his hand as he stepped closer to Lydia. He brushed up against her back, covering her from behind. Better. Much better.

Then he checked out the others in the room. Two young boys, one Slade and the other who must be Tate, sat quietly talking. He scanned the remaining space, but all was clear.

Brigs jabbed him in the arm. "A word please. Over there."

With a frown, he followed Brigs across the room, joined him and pressed his back against the wall. Lydia sat beside Colt's wife and hugged her. "What's up?"

"You're asking me? We have to maintain a low profile, and you plastered against Lydia's back isn't doing that."

"I wasn't plastered. It's called protection."

The elevator doors pinged open and an older man strode in. The man surveyed the area, his gaze clashing with theirs between one step and the next. Uh-huh, this was Ronson Brown, his actions ringing of Force, or ex-Force as Lydia had said he now was.

Ronson continued toward Lydia. She jumped to her feet and gave her supposed uncle a fierce hug. They appeared close. Tyler couldn't halt his low growl.

Then Ronson leaned in and whispered in her ear. She nodded and whispered back, her shoulders slumping a little.

Damn it. Jealousy slapped him hard in the gut. He didn't care to have his woman whisper to, and trust another man, in any way, and certainly not when it was him he wanted her to come to.

"Hey, no." Brigs's slammed a hand over his chest, barring him from moving. "You're so readable right now, and Ronson will come to us. You know he will. Wait it out."

Lydia. She looked so pale and shaken, as if she needed him ten-times over. Then she looked at him and her gaze softened. He itched for closer contact.

Brigs lowered his hand. "They're coming. Keep your cool."

They crossed the room, leaving the others behind. Her chest rose and fell with short breaths as she came to him. "Ronson." Her tone was low. "As you guessed, this is Tyler. With him is Brigs."

Okay, good. Ronson somehow knew who he was.

"I've heard plenty about you, Tyler."

"I've heard very little about you." Still, he stuck his hand out and they shook.

"We can't talk here. Come up to the homestead later."

"We'll bring our bags."

Ronson lifted a brow then placed his hand on Lydia's elbow. "Like I said, we'll talk later. Excuse us." He drew her away.

Tyler's control snapped. Ronson was taking her from him. No one would ever do that again. Not on his watch.

Brigs whipped around and blocked his way. "C'mon, snap out of it. She's right here in this room. She's not going anywhere. Although, you should. Go and walk it off."

He wanted to hold his girl the way he needed to and couldn't, yet with no choice, he turned and walked away, because it was either that or expose Lydia.

Down the hallway, he found a small room, one with a wooden cross on it marking it as a place to pray. He walked into the solitary space and chose the furthest of the four wooden pews where a small window above it overlooked the rooftops to the road.

He dropped to the bench and scrubbed a hand along his thigh.

What a mess.

And another shooting, one far too close to Lydia for his comfort. Yeah, he had to get control of this situation, which meant— His cell phone vibrated in his pocket.

He hauled it out and stared at the display. Ben. A call he couldn't miss. "Hey."

"Brigs just sent me a message. It said you wanted to go under. Isn't there another way?"

"No. Lydia's pregnant. I'm staying where she is."

"Look, you'll always have our support, but I want you to consider all your options. We can keep any visits you make there on the down low. I've worked with Ronson in the past. It was a few years ago, but I could speak to him."

He'd never ask Ben to cross such a line. "It's fine. Occasional visits with Lydia won't cut it for me at this point."

"Right, then at least let me get you a day or two. I'll tell Ronson you need to speak to your family. You certainly can't go under and leave me with the Whitehall brothers breathing down my neck. There's only so much I can handle."

"They will be pissed." He'd be lucky if his brothers allowed this to pass, except they'd have no choice. Once he was under, they'd never find him.

"Yeah, I can just see the three of them taking me down, one after the other. And it won't be pretty." Ben whistled under his breath. "Okay, enough of that. Brigs told me about your flameout. I want a report, and I want it now."

"I'll get it to you tonight."

"Good. I told Brigs about this, and I'll update you too. I have news about the hacker who dropped the information about Lydia to the reporter. Our systems specialist has tracked the informant's routed computer IP address to one M. Taita of Wellington." He snarled. "Johnny was Mia Taita's younger brother and she's on the board of Taita Software, intending to take over once Taita Senior retires."

His head swam with the new feed of intel. "I know the Taita family wants answers on Johnny's death, but to place the only eyewitness in a vulnerable position is not the way to do it."

"I agree. No matter how desperate, giving the killer easy access to Lydia's name through that article has only placed her life on the line. I'll deal with Mia Taita personally, but first I need to sort Saria's re-identification now her finals are done. I'll catch a flight to Wellington in a couple of days once she's gone under. Until then, both you and Brigs need to stay alert."

"Will do." Tyler ended the call and rubbed his shoulder. The tension within him had his back knotted tight. Hell, he'd have to leave Lydia for a short time to see his brothers, and he would, but only because Brigs was here. That conversation with his brothers wasn't one he looked forward to.

Chapter 14

They'd all been given two minutes with Drake after he'd stirred, but he'd been so drowsy, his mumbled words made little sense. The nurse had sent them out, assuring them he'd be more lucid in the morning.

That evening at the homestead, Lydia fidgeted with the dining table's lace runner trailing into her lap. Her nerves were shot.

Lifting her head, she focused on the conversation around the table. Between Tyler and Brigs, they'd both outlined to Ronson the depth of their involvement in her case.

Ronson listened, his arms crossed in front of him. "I understand you two men have Jenna's best interests at heart, but Drake's shooting had nothing to do with her. I'm responsible for her safety, and for adhering to The Program's strict re-identification guidelines."

"Someone got shot on your property," Tyler argued. "Her environment is not safe. We need to stay. Have you spoken to Ben Hammers yet?"

"He called." Ronson tapped along his arms. "Look, the best I can do is request you aid me in safeguarding this station until I can call Gilchrist. I have to do that within twenty-four hours or risk my standing."

"I appreciate the offer. I'll take it."

Damn. So, she had a single day to come up with a plan to ensure Tyler didn't give up his family for her. It wasn't nearly enough time.

"Hey." He caught her hand and gave it a squeeze. "I'll sort things with my brothers."

"Great. You do that." She was so not on board.

Ronson scraped his chair back as he rose. "Lydia will show you to your rooms, and if there's anything you need, my door is always open." To her, he said, "I'm taking a quick trip to the crossing. I know the area better than any detective, and I want to make sure nothing was missed in their preliminary search."

"I'll come with you if you don't mind." Brigs joined him.

"Not a problem."

They left and Tyler tugged her to her feet. "I need a laptop to compile my report for Ben."

"It's in the office at the back of the house."

"C'mon, I need to bring it out here where you'll be. Show me the way."

"I'm going upstairs to make the spare beds." She put emphasis on the word "beds."

"You're angry at me?"

"I won't take you away from your family. I can't do it."

"I'm not happy about leaving them either, but I've tried living without you, and it's not working for me."

As she backed up, her shoulders hit the wall. "I know how much you love your brothers. Think of Nico. I can't let him go through the pain of losing another family member. He's just a boy."

He prowled after her. "You're pregnant, and I won't allow my child to be raised without me."

"That's several months away. Hold off on your decision. You have to see that's possible."

"No."

"You're not being practical. No matter what happens, I'll

call you and we'll work out how to meet without you losing your family. You have to consider what I ask."

"What kind of life is that? I might have my family, but I get slim pickings with you." He slid his hand over her belly. "We're not going to argue about this anymore. Point the way to the office so I can grab the laptop and get some work done. I'd like to use the dining table. It's central. I can see the back door, the kitchen and the living room from here."

She turned on her heel and strode down the hallway. At Ronson's chunky desk, she jabbed a finger at the laptop. "Right there."

"Thank you." He took it and followed her back to the dining room. He set it on the table and fired it up. "Is there an exit or entry point from the upstairs floor?" He dragged a chair out and sat.

"No. The only way to leave the second level is by the stairs behind you."

"That's good." He waved a hand in a rolling motion. "You go do whatever you need to. I'll be able to keep an eye on you from here. I'll be two hours, tops."

That had been three hours ago.

Shivering in bed, she squinted through the dark at the alarm clock on her bedside table. The red light flickered the midnight hour.

Moonlight traced into the room through the sheer white nets, playing the lacy pattern over her cream bedcovers and the plain-papered walls bordered with tiny yellow flowers.

Where was he?

Even Brigs and Ronson had returned from the crossing and popped in to check on her before heading to bed. They'd told her they'd found size twelve shoe imprints three-hundred yards from the expected location of where the shot was fired. Evidence missed, so they were going back tomorrow to widen their search. They believed the shooter had dashed through the trees a little ways on foot.

Ah, finally, heavy footsteps on the landing outside her bedroom.

The door creaked open, and a sliver of light from the hallway beamed in.

She turned on the side lamp then pulled her knees to her chest as she sat up. "Did you get your report done?"

He yawned and shut the door. "Yeah. I had to finish it since I need to see my brothers first thing. I've booked a round trip to Auckland, but I'll be back by five tomorrow night. Brigs will watch you like a hawk until I get back." Muscles rippled across his chest as he raised the hem of his white shirt over his head. Yum. She wanted to lick his wicked bare skin.

"So, you're still going ahead with this?"

"Yes." He shucked off his pants and crawled in beside her. Flopped on his back, he stared at the ceiling. "You're not changing my mind."

She rolled onto her side and touched a finger to the shadows under his eyes. Today had certainly taken a physical toll on him. "You are so stubborn. You could have your brothers and me. I hate you can't see that."

"I'm glad you're not tossing me out of your bed." He grasped her hand and tucked it over his chest then with another yawn, he shut his eyes.

"Ha. You wouldn't go if I tried."

He smiled. "Finally, you understand me."

"Go to sleep. You look exhausted."

"It was difficult to put my lost images into order, but now it's done. I'll be fine come morning."

"Can I see your report?"

"Tomorrow." With another wide yawn, he rolled to his side.

She waited as his breathing evened out.

Slowly, she slid her fingers from his and slunk out of bed. She wanted to see his report, and it wouldn't wait until morning.

On tiptoes, she snuck down the stairs.

The laptop sat on the dining table and she opened the last working document. Bingo.

Reading the report, she covered each detailed account, from the moment Tyler had arrived at Jeffrey Lawntree's to the time of his shooting. There were discussions of interest he'd had with Lawntree, ones held late at night after she'd gone to bed.

Also, personal thoughts and opinions, although none of them surprised her. Lawntree was a politician, one whose career was his life. There was nothing she hadn't already alluded to in her own reports to both the police and those in The Program.

Damn. She'd hoped something within Tyler's report might mean something to her, perhaps even trigger a misplaced thought, but nothing.

She closed the lid and rubbed her forehead. She needed some space and clear air, somewhere quiet where she could consider her options, ones Tyler was eliminating one by one. Glancing up the stairwell, all was still clear.

She padded barefoot to the mudroom, grabbed a jacket from the hook, and pulled it over her pink camisole and sleep shorts. It wasn't cold out, but the wind was brisk as she followed the pebbled path highlighted by the moon's glow. It led around the side of the homestead. She scaled the wooden stile over the wire fence and hopped into the back field. All was dark, but in the light of day, long blades of green grass would ripple in the breeze.

This was the most beautiful spot on the station. A majestic maple tree spread its wide branches in the center of the meadow, and she lay beneath it. She linked her hands behind her head and stared at the thick blanket of midnight sky. Millions of diamond-like stars twinkled.

Her sister loved the night sky, just as she did. If Saria were here, she'd be outside with her, but instead she was hundreds of miles away, preparing for her own re-identification now her finals were done.

Tears streamed down her face. Tyler would have to deal with these emotions too, if she couldn't make him take back his decision. His brothers would be furious. Tyler didn't need to go under. Why didn't he see that? He was so obstinate.

Which meant plan, and she had to come up with one to make things right.

A metallic twang echoed on the breeze.

She rolled to her side, but saw no one crossing the stile. A shiver chased down her spine. Farther down the fence, a very large someone climbed between the wires. The cloaked man held a long rifle, the metal shone in the moonlight. Nobody on this station would carry a weapon in the dark of night.

Her heart jumped then skittered out of time.

She rolled to her front and flattened to the ground. No, bad move. Lying low would let this man get to the homestead. Making the only decision she could, to take control, she leapt to her feet.

The man from the phone booth twisted toward her. "Well, looky there," Ladd Hyena leered as he trained his rifle on her. "Just the person I was after."

Hell.

* * * *

As a gunshot ricocheted across the valley, Tyler jackknifed out of bed. He made a grab for Lydia, except she wasn't there.

He bellowed her name as he jammed his legs into his pants and snatched his weapon. At the top landing, Brigs and Ronson bounded half-dressed from their rooms and joined him, guns in hand. Tyler's heartbeat pummeled his chest. "I don't know where she is."

Racing down the stairs, Brigs led the way. "Let's go. That gunshot was close."

They all called to her, except nothing.

Where was she?

Outside the three of them halted, remaining deathly quiet.

Ronson leaned in. "The gunshot came from downhill. We'll separate and search. Stay low."

Tyler was off. This was his worst nightmare. What would make Lydia leave the house in the middle of the night? And damn it, this homestead was her safe location. What had happened to that?

Over the stile he went, and Ronson and Brigs dropped in beside him. They slithered into the darkness. On his belly, he combat-crawled in a zigzag path through the long grass, alert to any movement or noise.

As he tracked downhill, Brigs closed in on his right and Ronson on his left.

"I hear voices near the bushes," Brigs warned, the whites of his eyes gleaming.

"It's a man and a woman's," Ronson added.

Swift and precise, they eased under the wire fence and crawled into the next field. His elbows were raw, the gun in his hand primed and ready to fire. No one would take Lydia from him and survive.

Near the fringe of thicket, she was being shoved to her knees.

A sneering man stood over her, the barrel of his rifle exposed. "This spot farther away will do."

"Give me something. It's not as if I can hurt you." Her words were strong, but her voice wobbled.

"Ha, it was a stroke of luck seeing you at the pumps with the kid. Drake's old lady told me where she'd hunted her kid's address to, and I came up here the next day. I saw you and Drake having a chat on the porch, and I pulled the boss's hit pic of you out of my pocket and stripped away the disguise."

"That's how you found me? But why shoot Drake?"

"That stupid brat. I followed Drake and that other kid to the river. I dealt with Drake first. To let him know his father's serious about needing his kidney. My nephew will come around better now. He'll know nothing else will fly but his agreement. Then I came back for you, only you'd disappeared in that truck of yours." He stroked his rifle. "A bit of a pain that, but I'm getting the deed done now. I'm certainly not gonna cart you all the way to Wellington to let my boss see to his business. He'll want you gone after a year of looking for you."

"Who wants me dead? Who's your boss?" She shook where she knelt.

Damn it, he couldn't stand this, no matter the shooter's answer was crucial to solving her case.

"He's the head, and no one you know." The shooter smirked. "Say nighty-night."

That was it. Tyler pulled the trigger the same second as Brigs did.

The killer arched his back, the impact blowing his breath from his lungs. His knees buckled and his rifle slid to the ground. He collapsed and Lydia screamed.

Tyler raced to her. Hunched over, she gasped for air as he pulled her into his arms. "Are you hurt?"

"I couldn't let him get to you. He was here for me."

"What about the shot I heard?"

"It whizzed past me and hit the maple tree. He wanted to take me to his boss, the one who killed Johnny Taita. He dragged me down here." Her eyes bulged wide as she stared at the gunman. "He's Ladd Hyena, Drake's uncle."

"We'll find out everything we need to know about him. He can't hurt you anymore."

"No, Tyler." She thumped his chest, shaking her head. "The man who murdered Johnny Taita's still out there. Didn't you hear him? He said his boss has been searching for me. This is never going to end."

"This idiot may have come for you, but look how he's leaving." Stroking her hair, he tucked her closer. He glanced at

Brigs kneeling over Hyena. "Is he dead?"

"No, he's breathing." Brigs heaved his cell phone from his pocket. "I guess we can't interrogate a dead man. I'll call emergency services."

Ronson's eyes were flat. "If Hyena moves a muscle, I'll take it as a sign he's going for his weapon."

The same went for Tyler.

Brigs nodded. "I'll call Ben and get him here."

"I can't believe I brought Jenna right into a hornet's nest." Ronson dropped to his haunches and checked the gunman's pockets. "I had no idea Drake's uncle was after him, and of any possible cross-over like this."

Lydia fisted her hands against Tyler's chest. "Who's his boss?"

Her words were a fearful cry, ones which made his blood curdle. "We'll find out. We won't rest until we do."

She burrowed her head into his shoulder, and one very precise fact blared at him. He would have lost all reason to live had she died this night. Her very essence was branded into him like fire.

"Let me take you inside, love." He pressed a kiss to the top of her head.

Tears swam in her eyes as she lifted her chin. "The one who killed Johnny will come. H-he'll know where I am."

"You'll be moved, and no one will ever get through me to you. I promise you."

"That's exactly my problem." Her eyelids fluttered and she went slack in his arms.

He scooped her up as she lost consciousness, bent and checked her breathing.

She was fine. Just fainted, which considering all she'd gone through, wasn't a surprise. Hell. He needed to take her away from all this, to where only he would know where she was. "No one takes you from me, Lee." He whispered the solemn promise as he strode back to the homestead with her in his arms. "We stay together. Forever."

With his last breath, he'd make that happen.

Chapter 15

Lydia woke with a jump, recalling all that had happened and barely swallowing her tears of panic.

"You're safe." Tyler cupped her face. "We're in your room."

The first streaks of blood-red dawn lit the sky. A bare few hours ago, a man had come to kill her, and had almost succeeded.

She shuddered as ice flowed through her veins. Tyler had rescued her, but what if the killer had made it inside? Again Tyler's life would have been placed on the line because of her.

"D-did he survive?"

"Yes, he's out of surgery. Gilchrist flew in and is waiting at the hospital. He's keeping us updated of any developments. Ben came in by chopper at dawn, and he's downstairs with Ronson."

"Who's looking after Saria?"

"Mathias." He pried open her fingers and rubbed her hands. "She's completely safe. It's you I'm worried about."

"I want to get up."

Gilchrist, her new handler, was likely her only ally. Wriggling, she tried to break free, but he lay half over her, pinning her to the bed.

"You need to stay put." His kiss seared her cold lips. "Or if you feel like moving, then let me make love to you."

Melting into him, she ached to say yes, only she had to get to Gilchrist. "Take me to the hospital."

"Ah, my Lee, that was a bad answer. I'm going to undress you. Say yes." He caressed her sides down to the hem of her pink camisole, drew it over her head and tossed it to the carpet.

"I didn't say yes."

"You want to undress me, love?" His voice was a purr as he nuzzled between her bare breasts and cupped both mounds, so full and aching for his touch.

"Ah, no." She tore her gaze from his rippling, tanned pecs.

"Then I'll do it." Grinning, he popped the button on his Levis, slid them down his thighs thick with muscle and off.

Oh, pure bliss. Her man was beautiful, and every hard and cut inch of him demanded she explore and touch.

"I'll always be here." Naked, he knelt on the satin sheets between her legs, lowered her hands to the bare skin of her belly and covered them with his own. "With you and our child."

"Tyler, you don't fight fair."

"I don't want to fight at all. I'm still waiting for my yes." Lust filled his gaze as he tugged her pink pajama shorts down. With painstaking slowness, he trailed a finger from her neck to her navel, sending a torrent of delicious tingles spiraling out. "My mouth is watering for a taste."

"I love it when you touch me like that."

"That's my girl. Now say yes." He lowered his head and kissed her heated skin from her neck to her breasts. He plucked one nipple, while sucking the other.

Arching her back, she pushed her so sensitive breast deeper into his mouth. "Yes. You can definitely have your yes."

"Perfect. I can't wait to feast." He gripped her legs and spread them, revealing all of her to his hungry gaze.

A thrill chased through her and she slid her legs against his.

He ducked his head and she tangled her hands deep into his black hair, holding onto him as his tongue lashed across her flesh.

Breathless, heart soaring, she clung to him. "Slow down."

"That doesn't work for us." Lapping at her, he built her orgasm to a pinnacle until she had nowhere to go but over the edge. She could never say no to him, and as she exploded, flashes of white and gold burst behind her closed lids, burning through her as she came, over and over. His very scent became hers, entrenched in her skin. Too much, yet not enough.

"You want me inside?"

"You know I do."

Breathing raggedly, he rubbed his cock over her clit and plunged into her.

Biting back a scream, she locked him in place. Her channel greedily seized him, squeezing and demanding more as he rode her.

He jerked deep inside her as he came, sending her skyward with him. Pleasure radiated from the tips of her fingers to the ends of her toes.

"I love you, Lee. You are my world, and that will never change." He covered her mouth with his, kissing her as he stroked her face and rocked gently inside her. Slowly, he brought them both back down.

"Tyler." She couldn't get more than his name out since he'd stolen her last lungful of air with his words of love.

"Mmm," he murmured, his cock twitching and lengthening again deep inside her. "Are you trying to tell me you're ready for round two?"

"No, we've barely finished round one."

"Wrong answer."

Heck, he always had to have his way. "How about we take a shower first? Then I'll give you a yes."

He rolled her off the soft mattress, scooped her up then carried her to her bathroom. "How about we do both at the same time. I love taking showers with you, and it's been too long.

Round two is about to begin."

One very pleasurable cleaning later, she came out of the shower barely able to stand. He had the most ferocious appetite.

"We really need to check in with Brigs and Ben, and I can't do that if I don't take my hands off you. Go dress while I shave, okay?" He drew a towel around her and patted her bottom.

"Sure. I won't be long." She padded to her painted dresser, pulled on a pair of skinny white jeans, and topped them with a red cap-sleeved t-shirt. From the bedside table, she took her dreaded glasses and slid them on. He loved her, and she had every intention of going behind his back and returning to Gilchrist.

She trudged back to the bathroom and eyed his broad back down to the fleecy blue towel slung low on his hips. She so wanted to take that towel off, and stay naked with him for the rest of the day. Right now, her life sucked.

"Um, I truly need to get to the hospital and see Drake." Tucking her hair behind one ear, she met his blue gaze in the mirror as he shaved. "We've gotten close."

"That depends on what the plan is. We'll talk to Ben first, and see what's going on. He'll be waiting downstairs." He finished up, removed his towel and slung it over the rail on his way to the bedroom.

She drooled at all his gorgeous golden skin, and one very stiff cock ready for more of her. Only she had to get her mind on the right track. Could she make him see reason? "I want you safe."

"I know, and I want you with me." He tugged on a pair of tight jeans and a black silk shirt. From his bag, he took his holster, strapped it on and slotted his gun inside. "And that will only happen if I go through re-identification with you, as your partner."

Gripping her hand, he led her from of the room.

His mind was set, but then so was hers. Sooner or later

she'd get her way. She had to.

* * * *

Tyler guided Lydia downstairs, her current silence a dire warning. He'd watch her for any sign of flight. From the living room, the others' voices rose. He couldn't lag behind on any information. Lydia's safety depended on it.

He strode into the large room where Ronson and Ben stood before a coffee table scattered with files.

Ronson looked Lydia over. "How are you feeling?"

"Better than last night." She hugged him, and then eyed Ben. "How's Saria?"

Ben gripped her shoulder. "She's not happy I had to leave, and she guessed it was to do with you. I told her I'd sort this."

"Saria will be fine. It's you we need to watch." Tyler led her to the couch.

"That's right." Ben took a seat opposite them. "Let's cover this new information that's come to hand."

Ronson took a file from the coffee table and passed it across. "Ben brought a full report on Drake's uncle. As we're now aware, the man's name is Ladd Hyena, forty-two of Wellington. He's affiliated with a large gang and we're running checks on who his boss could be. Take a look at what I've given you."

Tyler scanned the file as Lydia leaned against him and read along. Ladd Hyena's parents were deceased, and he had an older brother named Kern, Drake's father. Ladd had been arrested for all manner of things, the most prominent armed robbery. He'd spent a few years in jail, but had been released four years ago.

Ben rubbed his jaw. "Gilchrist is waiting for the doctor's permission to interview Hyena. He also intends to chat with Drake since he's Hyena's first victim."

Ronson gritted his teeth. "The Hyena family is into heavy gang stuff, but not Drake. His father and uncle dumped him two years ago at the site of a shooting, which is how Drake ended up in juvie. Drake had no one. I took on his case and offered to track down his mother for him, but Drake wouldn't give me her name. She abandoned him, and he wants nothing to do with her. He wanted to make a clean break from them all."

"He had until now." Lydia gripped Tyler's thigh, her nails digging in.

He clasped his hand over hers. "Hyena came here for Drake, doing his brother a favor, and found Lydia by chance. In the field, Hyena said his boss killed Johnny Taita."

Ben nodded. "Yes, which gives us the strongest link we've ever had in Johnny Taita's case. We have to check every single angle of this cross-over, and locate Hyena's boss, which means going to the source, Ladd Hyena."

Lydia jumped to her feet. "If you're going to the hospital, I'm coming."

Yeah, she was after Gilchrist plain and simple. Tyler's gut rolled with the knowledge.

Ben eyed her. "You'll remain under strict guard when you come, and only because I want Tyler and Brigs with me and this homestead isn't safe. Gilchrist will also want you moved, and it will be easier to take you to him." He glanced at Ronson. "You okay with that?"

"Of course. Keep her safe." Ronson rose and gave Lydia a hug. "I want you to take the utmost care. Don't get shot at again."

"I won't." Her words were muffled into his black-checked shirt. "Thank you for looking after me the way you have."

A tear escaped Ronson's eyes as he patted her back. "You're family, and no matter where you are, never forget I'm here for you."

"C'mon." Tyler took her hand. "Let's feed you so we can leave." He led the way to the kitchen. "What would you like?"

"I don't think I can eat, not right now."

"For our little one, you have to." He hauled out a chair from the table for two tucked in the corner under a wooden shuttered window and sat her in it. From the pantry he chose a box of cereal and set it on the table. He fetched bowls and milk, returned and took a seat.

"You haven't been to see your brothers. Now you'll miss your flight." Her hands twitched in the folds of the tablecloth.

"Hey, don't worry about it."

"I can't help it." She left her seat and slid onto his lap. Pressing her lips to his, she kissed him as her tears fell. "I love you, Tyler, more than my own heart can even stand. I've wanted to tell you for so long."

"As I love you. We'll sort this." His chest tightened painfully, almost squeezing in on itself.

She was his life, and he'd never allow the killer who was after her to take her. No one would ever harm her again. Cupping her face, he kissed her back, losing himself in the taste of her. "You're mine."

Chapter 16

All the way to the hospital, Lydia puzzled every possible angle open to her. Sure they had more leads now in Johnny Taita's case, but that wouldn't stop Gilchrist from seeing her moved again before the day was out. And she was committed to making certain Tyler didn't lose his brothers.

Gunnar met them at the main entrance. He remained behind her, Ben ahead, and Tyler and Brigs hemmed her in on either side as they strode in.

Gunnar would be the perfect addition to her plan. At first she'd thought to get Gilchrist alone, but Tyler was too smart not to know she'd try that. No, Gunnar was Gilchrist's partner, but not her handler. If she could get him on her side, she might be able to convince him to move her on his own, and leave Tyler behind. She had to speak to Gunner, and without Tyler catching on.

In the wide corridor to the elevators, people darted out of their way. She would too if these four fierce looking men strode her way. They were all outfitted in black, and she wore the bulletproof vest Tyler had insisted on underneath her shirt.

Gunnar pressed the button for the top floor and they traveled up. The doors swished open, and a uniformed officer stepped forward to check them over. He nodded at Gunnar and sent them through.

When they passed the nurses' station, Gunnar stopped and faced them. "We can't commandeer an entire ward, but we've got Ladd Hyena and Drake secured in separate rooms at the end of this corridor. Hyena has an officer posted inside and outside his room, and Drake has a guard with him. Only legitimate visitors who have family can get into this ward, but as you can see, it's fairly clear."

She rubbed her arms as she checked out the waiting room. A woman in her mid-forties sat hunched in a metal-legged chair, her head between her palms. An officer sat beside her.

Tyler pressed a hand to the small of her back then ran his thumb over the vest under her shirt. "This is where you'll wait."

"Sure." She hadn't expected him to let her anywhere near Hyena. She turned to Gunnar. "Who's she?" For some reason, even with her face downcast, the woman with the dark messy hair looked familiar.

"She's Drake's mother and she arrived from Wellington this morning. We let her in to see her son, although the reception didn't go well. Drake screamed at her to leave. A detective's chatting with Drake now, and then coming back to question her. An officer is sitting with her because of the earlier disturbance. Every precaution is being taken."

"Drake said he doesn't want anything to do with his mother. She gave Hyena Drake's address."

"Yes, the lady's already admitted to that, but she said she had no idea why Hyena wanted it. She said Drake was Kern's boy, not hers. She thought she was being helpful. A detective will interview her formally, and she's agreed to wait." Gunnar looked over her shoulder. "Ah, here's Gilchrist."

Gilchrist strode toward them, extending his hand to Ben. "Good to see you. I can only say I appreciate your team's arrival, no matter it took me by surprise. All issues aside, it's my client's safety that comes first, and we have Ladd Hyena under heavy guard. He's woken, and his doctor has confirmed he's of sound mind to be interviewed. We're all set if you'd like in."

"Yes we would." Ben turned to Gunnar. "Do you mind if we commandeer you to keep an eye on Jenna? There's no one else we trust."

"No problem. She won't leave my sight, and this ward has several officers posted within."

Tyler slapped Gunnar's shoulder. "She's also not to leave this building, or this floor. She doesn't speak to anyone, and you don't listen to any request she makes to go through re-identification without me. If she tries to bring up the subject, I want to know." Tyler's gaze sharpened on hers. "Have I covered everything?"

Jeez, she hated how efficient he was.

"Yeah, sure. Idiot."

Brigs chuckled. "Sorry, inappropriate."

Tyler ran a finger under her chin. "Take a seat with Gunnar. I'll be back before you know it."

"I'm sure you will. If I holler, make sure you come." With a huff, she turned on her heel and followed Gunnar to the waiting room where he chose seats in the far corner.

"Gunnar, I'd still like to talk about re-identification." She crossed her legs as she sat.

"Are you trying to get me into trouble? I heard your man."

"Yeah, but I'm the client, not Tyler. Would you at least hear me out?"

"I'll give you one minute."

She straightened, rubbing her hands together.

"Wait. I hear someone." His gaze shot to entrance. A detective strode in. "Nope, he's fine. He'll be here to interview Drake's mother."

The detective raised a silver badge and flashed it Gunnar's way before heading across to Drake's mother. The woman eyed the detective, her mouth twisting to the side.

Whoa. Something about the woman was still infinitely

familiar. Sure, she had the same slanted eyes as Drake and high cheekbones, but there was more. It was as if she'd seen her before.

The detective cleared his throat. "Ma'am, I've spoken to your son, and you've given me conflicting information. Your name is not what you told us."

The lady stood and shoved her hands on her hips. "I agreed to an interview. I know I gave Ladd Hyena Drake's address, but that's not a crime. Drake's father wanted it, so I found it."

"Your son says your word's not trustworthy. Give me your name."

"Of course he'd say that, but he's completely screwed up. As it is, he's been in juvie and he's only eighteen."

Why on earth had she even come here when she clearly didn't care about Drake?

She stood and took a step toward the woman. "Drake's a friend of mine. Who are you? Why have you come?"

Drake's mother spun and faced her, her gaze zeroing in. "You!"

Holy moly, she'd stood behind Taita Senior in the news footage Brigs had sent. How the hell was Taita Senior's daughter Drake Hyena's mother?

The woman screeched and lunged toward her.

Gunnar dived and tackled her.

Obscenities flew, her shrieks pinging against the walls. She kicked and clawed for her freedom.

Tyler sprinted into the room, Brigs, Ben and Gilchrist right behind him. He ran to her and hauled her into his arms. "What's going on?"

"Drake's mother is Taita Senior's daughter. Drake said she was into computers, but I never thought like this."

His hold tightened like steel on her as he scrutinized the woman. "Mia Taita leaked your information to the reporter."

"This is such a mess. The entire family was cleared of any

involvement at the beginning. Certainly none of them matched my description, but—" She clapped a hand to her mouth. "Oh my goodness. Kern Hyena needs a kidney transplant. He's not family."

"Damn it, you said the gunman had yellowish skin."

"I never connected it to kidney failure."

Drake's mother's fought Gunnar. "Get off me. I want access to a phone. I want to call my lawyer. Now."

"You're not going anywhere, lady." Gunnar kept her face planted to the ground and his knee shoved into her back as the detective cuffed her.

She screamed, her gaze wild on Lydia's. "I can't believe you're here."

"Why Drake? Why are you here?"

Her gaze spat fire. "I promised Kern I'd find out where Drake was and I did, but he won't stop using me until he has that boy's kidney."

No wonder Drake wanted nothing to do with her. "I hope you rot in hell. Drake deserves better than you."

"It's not illegal to find someone. I've done nothing wrong, and I'll have my lawyer prove it." Her cuffs rattled as she yanked on them.

"Just save it." Gunnar heaved her around and pulled her to the doors. The detective followed Gunnar from the room.

Like sentinels, Ben and Gilchrist surrounded her and Tyler.

She shook, all that had happened hitting her hard.

"Here's Taita's purse." Brigs leaned over the chair the woman had sat in and snatched it up. He tossed it to Ben.

Ben riffled through it and held up her driver's license. "Definitely Mia Taita." He eyed Gilchrist. "Guess where we're going?"

"To locate and lock up Kern Hyena." Gilchrist clapped Tyler on the shoulder. "I could use your help. I'm leaving you in charge of Jenna Winton's security. Once I have Kern Hyena in custody, and all the details sorted, I'll contact you to give you the all clear. In the meantime, stay low and out of sight."

"About damn time." Tyler jerked his head toward the elevators. "What are you still doing here? Get moving."

No sweeter words had she ever heard, and once they left, she kissed the man who'd issued them, not breaking for air until she needed it. "I want to go home, with you, but with one proviso on the staying low."

"Please tell me you want a big, big bed involved."

"Yes, and with you naked in it. For days on end."

"Ahh, we have the same thing in mind." He swung her up into his arms, grinning as he carried her from the room. "Finally we're in complete agreement."

Chapter 17

Digging her fingers into the silk sheet under her, Lydia held onto her thoughts by a mere thread. "Making love to you rocks."

"And I never want to stop." Tyler balanced over her as The Idle Dream cruised the Pacific Ocean.

She wrapped her arms around his neck. "What am I going to do with you?"

"I say we change your name one more time. Lydia Sands and Jenna Winton, no more. I want you to be Mrs. Whitehall."

"Did you just propose to me?"

"Call it what you will, but we're getting married either way."

She laughed, and then relaxed back with a sigh, secure in Tyler's arms.

So much had happened since they'd left Blenheim. Tyler had chartered a plane to Auckland, and during the flight Ben had linked in via video conference to confirm they had Kern Hyena in custody, and the man matched her description. He'd requested she take a look at Hyena and produced his mug shot for her to confirm his identity.

The killer's beady eyes drilled into her, his lips twisted in an evil snarl. His fury had jumped out, making her cringe back into her soft leather seat.

"Relax. It's just an image. Look at me." Tyler had lifted her hands and pressed them against the scorching heat of his chest, his gaze and hold piercingly protective. "No one will ever harm you again. Do you understand me? Ever. Again."

"Yes." She'd kissed him then faced Ben and nodded. "It's him. He's the one who killed Johnny Taita and shot Tyler. What's going to happen now?"

"Charges will be laid against Kern Hyena for everything Gilchrist can slap on him. Mia Taita's already lawyered up, although we're well aware she's the remaining heir to Taita Senior's company. Add to that she leaked your information to the reporter, and she's the killer's ex and her dealings with him, then her motivation ramps up. She had a part in this, likely ordering the kill. The team here won't rest until they prove that assumption is more than mere speculation."

"What about Ladd Hyena?"

"The evidence of his attempt on yours and Drake's life is solid." He eyed Tyler. "You'll be pulled in as a witness to what you heard when he attempted to take Lydia's life, as will Brigs and Ronson. There isn't a chance Hyena will see the light of day for years to come."

"I'll be there. Have you spoken to Taita Senior?"

"Yes. The news hit him hard, but at least he has the truth. He's also requested to meet his grandson, but Drake's not up for it yet. The doctor's just issued his release from hospital, and he's returning shortly straight into Ronson's care." He tipped his gaze back to her. "Drake wants to see you. I informed him the moment Tyler allows it, you'll be there."

"Tell him I'll call him, that I still want my ride."

Tyler growled under his breath. "Which will be some time away. Thanks, Ben. We'll chat later." He switched off the link and squeezed her hands. "Okay, we need to talk about your need to ride bikes."

"No." She smiled and pressed a finger to his lips. "We need to talk about you and the big bed—"

"Hey, come back to me." Tyler caressed her belly, holding her and their child close.

"Sorry, I'm here." She looked into his beautiful eyes, those of the man who'd stolen her heart. "Do you want to go and see the others?"

His family and hers were upstairs. Tyler had arranged for everyone to come. Nico had been beyond excited.

"After you give me your answer on the name change. I've decided I want to hear a yes."

"Yes. I love you, and I want to be Mrs. Whitehall, but I'd prefer it if you called me Lee."

"Lee." He tangled his hands in her hair. "I love you so much it hurts."

"Then let me help you fix that." Wriggling her bare bottom into the sheets, she grinned. He'd guarded her a year ago, and she had no doubt, he'd guard her and their child for the rest of their lives.

No more pain, not now they were together.

Mrs. Whitehall. Oh yeah, she would surely love her new name.

Love these characters and want more?

Don't miss the rest of this adventurous series from a *New York Times* Bestselling Author.

He will sacrifice anything to protect her.

Billionaire Bodyguards Series

Billionaire Bodyguard Attraction, Book One

Billionaire Bodyguard Boss, Book Two

Billionaire Bodyguard Fling, Book Three

JOANNE WADSWORTH

BILLIONAIRE BODYGUARD
Boss

COMING NEXT - Saria and Ben's Story

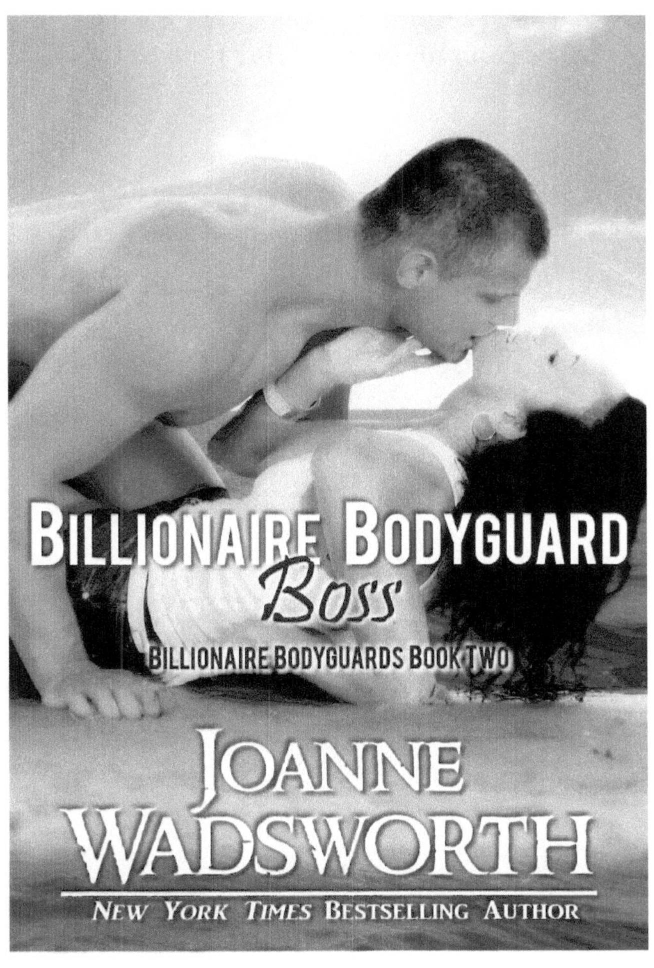

**Also available in paperback from this author —
Scottish Historical Romance**

There can only be one…for both of them.

The Matheson Brothers Series

Highlander's Desire, Book One

Highlander's Passion, Book Two

Highlander's Seduction, Book Three

JOANNE WADSWORTH

BILLIONAIRE BODYGUARD ATTRACTION

Highlander's Desire

The Matheson Brothers Series, Book One

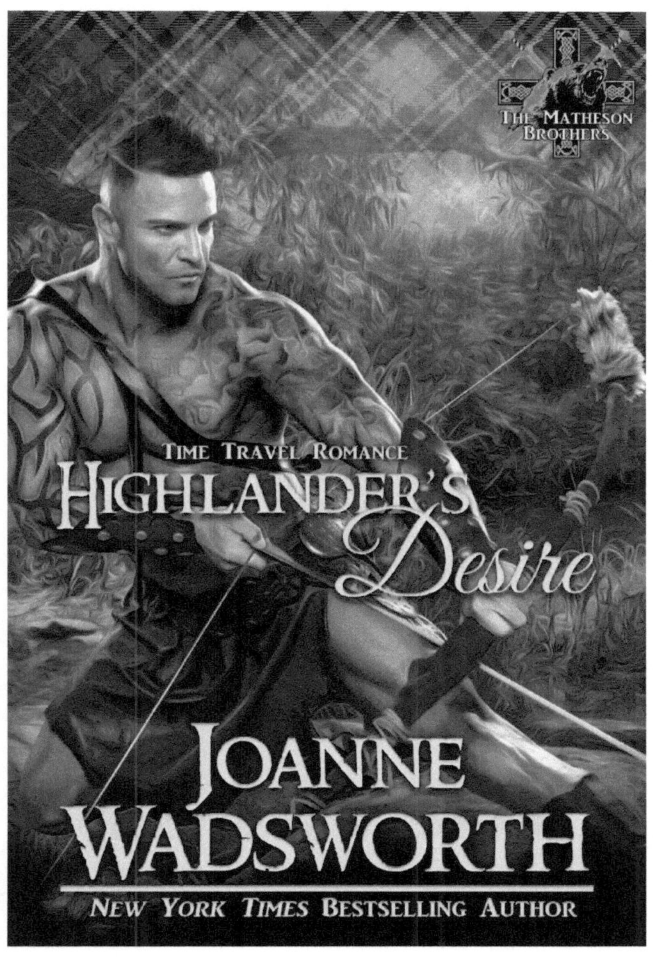

**Also available in paperback from this author —
Scottish Historical Romance**

Traveling through time…for a Highlander.

Highlander Heat Series

Highlander's Castle, Book One

Highlander's Magic, Book Two

Highlander's Charm, Book Three

Highlander's Guardian, Book Four

Highlander's Faerie, Book Five

Highlander's Champion, Book Six

JOANNE WADSWORTH

Highlander's Castle

Highlander Heat Series, Book One

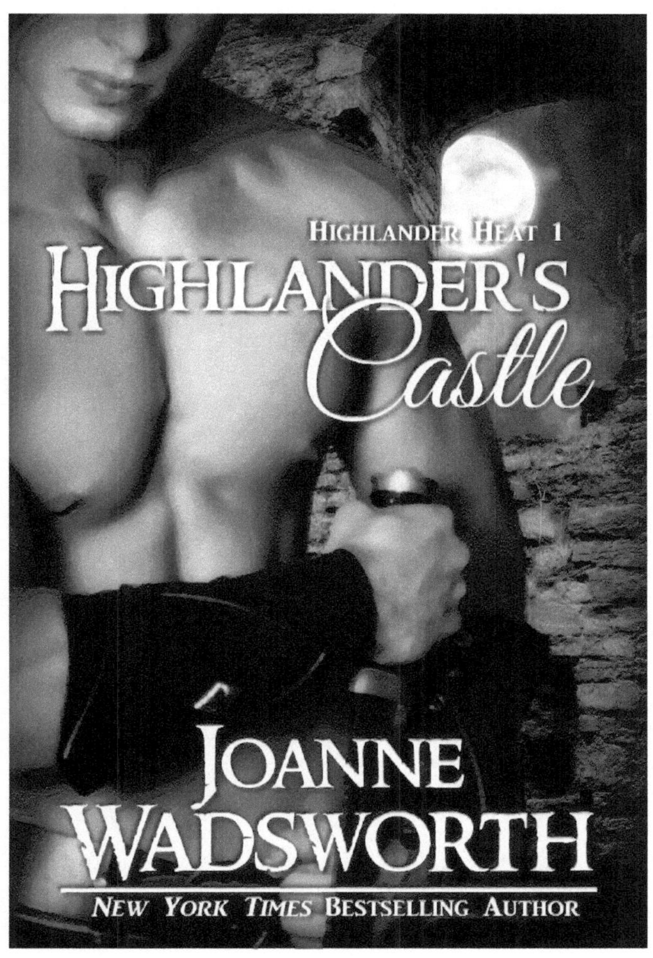

Don't miss this spell-binding Young Adult / New Adult Fantasy Romance series.

To love and protect…across worlds.

Princesses of Myth

Protector, Book One

Warrior, Book Two

Hunter, Book Five (Novella, Book 2.5)

Enchanter, Book Three

Healer, Book Four

Chaser, Book Five

JOANNE WADSWORTH

JOANNE WADSWORTH

Joanne Wadsworth is a *New York Times* and *USA Today* Bestselling Author who adores getting lost in the world of romance, no matter what era in time that might be. Hot alpha Highlanders hound her, demanding their stories are told and she's devoted to ensuring they meet their match, whether that be with a feisty lass from the present or far in the past.

Living on a tiny island at the bottom of the world, she calls New Zealand home. Big-dreamer, hoarder of chocolate, and addicted to juicy watermelons since the age of five, she chases after her four energetic children and has her own hunky hubby on the side.

So come and join in all the fun, because this kiwi girl promises to give you her "Hot-Highlander" oath, to bring you a heart-pounding, sexy adventure from the moment you turn the first page. This is where romance meets fantasy and adventure…

To learn more about Joanne and her works, visit:
Website and Blog
http://www.joannewadsworth.com